THE UNSELECTED JOURNALS OF *Emma M. Lion*

VOL. 1

BETH BROWER

THE UNSELECTED JOURNALS OF *Emma M. Lion*

VOL. 1

Rhysdon Press

This is a work of fiction. Names, characters, places and incidents either are the product of the author's imagination or are used fictitiously. Any resemblances to actual persons, living or dead, events, business establishments, or locales is entirely coincidental.

contact@rhysdonpress.com

Published by Rhysdon Press
Printed in the United States of America

Publishers Cataloging-in-Publication data. Brower, Beth.
The Unselected Journals of Emma M. Lion, Vol. 1: Beth Brower; p.cm.
ISBN 978-0-9980636-1-4 1. Fiction Historical 2. Fiction. I. Title.

10 9 8 7 6 5 4

978-0-9980636-1-4

Text was set in Baskerville

Emma M. Lion

would like to dedicate her journals to all those
who have the presumption to read them.

March 5th

I've arrived in London without incident.

There are few triumphs in my recent life, but I count this as one. My existence of the last three years has been nothing *but* incident.

The train billowed its way into St. Pancras Station five minutes early. Auspicious, as I am fairly certain such a thing has never before happened in the history of the British railway system. A less than enthusiastic porter helped me with my two trunks, my case, and my hat box. He took note of the frayed edges on my morning coat, made a sound of disapproval, and began to silently convey his displeasure at helping me. I did give him a halfpenny. *Rather* generous, considering my financial state. Strangely, it was the hat box that caused the greatest sneer, despite it actually carrying a hat. For over a year it carried something a modicum less pleasant: the monkey's head Maxwell sent me.

I almost crossed that out, the bit about the monkey's head. In Bournemouth, I developed a rather unfortunate habit of redaction, seeing as how Cousin Matilde was no respecter of personal belongings, as proven by The Great Burning of 1882. The tendency to assume I've no privacy has persisted despite my best efforts, but I am determined to break it. This journal does not deserve to have a foul, black mark running through every incriminating thought. I will no longer censor myself!

I digress.

After securing a hansom cab, an unavoidable expense, I gave the driver the directions to my favourite place in all the world:

Lapis Lazuli House in the neighbourhood of St. Crispian's, London.

My blessed fate.

As the cab turned onto Whereabouts Lane, I leaned out of the window to watch Lapis Lazuli House come into view. There it was! Tall and memorable, grey limestone with exterior carvings akin to a park bench or an ornate grave marker. When the cab rolled to a stop, I was out and onto the street, relieved to have finally arrived. Though the squared portico needs to be repainted, the five curved steps leading to the front door were newly swept. The windows need cleaning, but, dare I boast, they are taller than most in the neighbourhood. Yet, despite all this, there is an unaware feeling about this house that I love. As impressive as Lapis Lazuli is, it by no means takes itself over-seriously. A cosmic balance to the ego of its current inhabitant.

Cousin Archibald, said inhabitant, was not at home when I arrived. He must have sensed ~~his impending doom~~ my pending arrival. His man, Parian, was in, for it was he who answered the famous blue door and—after breathing out through his nose several disapproving times—allowed me to cross the sacred threshold. The new scullery-maid-turned-cook was also present for my arrival. Her name is Agnes. She is the most promising unpromising girl of sixteen I've ever met. Both she and Parian helped me transport my effects to my rooms.

There were several sets of stairs involved. Several. For my benevolent cousin has placed me not in my own rooms on the very reasonable third floor, but in the garret of the fifth floor.

The garret.

I repeat, the garret.

My old rooms are apparently mine no longer. I am banned from them. Why? one might ask. To which I answer, there are some things we are never meant to understand.

Though honesty demands I acknowledge it may have something to do with The Incident which led to The Scar.

Spitefully, the entire fourth floor is empty and is to remain untouched. The third floor consists of two guest bedrooms and my former rooms. Below that, Cousin Archibald occupies the second floor, including the forbidden-to-me library, which he keeps locked. The first floor hosts the drawing room, the dining room, and an unused salon. The kitchens and storerooms are on the ground floor, with a room for Agnes behind the kitchen, near the gardens.

Where, one might ask, resides Parian, our valet-turned-butler-turned-rather-intolerable-man? I carry my suspicions that His Current Rooms were formerly known as My Rooms. May he enjoy the view of the garden.

While this rearrangement might never have occurred in any other London household, I cannot say I am very surprised it has happened here. In the words of my maternal aunt, Lady Eugenia Spencer, "Lapis Lazuli is a bizarre establishment, to say the least." And she is never content to say the least, so let it be marked.

As for the state of the garret, it is a mess of furniture, dust, and cobwebs. Ascending the final staircase, one finds oneself presented with three doors. The left door opens to a west room, with one and a half windows that overlook the back garden. The middle door leads to a closet in severe disarray. The right door opens to the east room, also with one and a half windows, but that offer a view of the street. The half window is due to Lapis Lazuli Minor, which Cousin Archibald created when he walled off a ridiculously small, ten-foot sliver of the house in order to lure in wealthy renters. After giving a mere ten feet on every other floor—three of those ten feet being occupied by the former servants' stairway—Archibald waxed magnanimous in the garret and gave the flat full half. Meaning my rooms are smaller, and I have one and a half windows in each.

I have found a bed and a small night table among the detritus in the east room, and it is here I will make camp until I can assess the best course of action. Agnes made certain I understood that the bedding had been washed twice. She seemed so brightly insistent upon its cleanliness that I admit to feeling dimly alarmed as to what its previous state had been.

I did find, among the wreckage of the garret, a worn copy of *Paradise Lost*. Victory! Cousin Archibald's plan to keep me uneducated suffers a retreat. How wonderful it will be to have something to read until I can rebuild my own library. In addition, finding Milton in your garret must be a sign of sorts.

And so I say to myself, welcome home.

I shall have some cards made up.

Emma M. Lion
Lapis Lazuli House, Whereabouts Lane
London

March 6th

This morning I was informed that, unless otherwise directed, I would be taking all of my meals in my garret on a tray. Into the dining room I shall not go. Parian delivered the news with noticeable self-satisfaction. I believe my banishment has brought a great deal of joy to his life. I won't begrudge him it. He is, after all, Cousin Archibald's valet. Joy must not be easy for him to come by.

After he left, I considered this new dictum and its advantages to me. It's a grace to be sure, eating one's meal alone, outside the scrutiny of a crotchety old man. In celebration, while sitting pleasantly on my window seat, I ate some biscuits from the tin sent by Arabella.

I've always enjoyed the view from Lapis Lazuli, settled right on the elbow of Whereabouts Lane. It offers a perfect glance at anyone walking up or walking down, and the fifth-floor window has only improved it, the house stretching on tiptoe to capture the rooftops of London. Taking my meals here, while meant to be insult, will certainly cause no injury.

The one drawback about having my meals relegated to a tray in the garret (a good deal of poetic imagery there) is that I have neither purse nor scrip with which to slip out for a tea and baked goods as supplement to the comestibles fate sends forth from the kitchen. And everyone knows that those who live in garrets must find at least a portion of their sustenance from tea and baked goods at establishments such as Everett's or the Reed and Rite. It is immutable scientific fact. Perhaps Darwin wrote something on the subject. Speaking of, the man died in Kent last year. Kent! Survival of the fittest indeed. Considering his theories, perhaps I ought to go into Hyde Park and wrestle waif-like young ladies for their purses. London is a harsh climate and one must survive.

Cousin Archibald himself has not yet made an appearance, and thus I've had no chance to enquire after my owed salary and its accompanying allowance. My belief is that said salary and allowance has been on his mind also, my proof being his avoidance of me. I've seen a shadow of a man slip from the house in the early morning and slip back into the house in the late evening, and one can be quite sure that if it is a shadow of a man, it must be Cousin Archibald. He's not only thin in person, he's thin in humour and spirit and character.

I found a mirror in the west room and have moved it into the east room above the washstand. It must have been my great-aunt's and is beautifully framed in gold, a Greek key pattern as the adornment. Leaning it against the wall, it is tall enough to show the reality of my reflection.

I am looking rather pale.

Having seen Father in myself for so long, it is alarming to see Mother now. Father's eyes still belong to me, that uncanny sea green; wide-set, large, wholly disapproved of by Cousin Matilde.

But Mother has shown herself in a *tour de force.* I have her cheekbones, her way of raising my eyebrows, and the heritage of the women of this family: a dimpled chin. My hair is dark and unruly, a gift from my Portuguese maternal grandmother.

And across the bridge of my nose? A constellation of freckles.

"They will fade when you are older," Mother had said.

"I hope not," Father had called from across the room, bent over an illustration. "'Twould be a pity for Emma to lose that bit of magic, now wouldn't it?"

Well, Father, I haven't lost it, though I look in this mirror and recognise myself less now than when I was a child. I suppose that happens when you've grown up and still don't understand your place in the world.

By stature, I am neither very tall nor very short, but am fixed prosaically in between. Cousin Matilde once claimed this to be my single asset in finding a husband. "Men don't want a gawky, tall specimen, nor a stunted child, our Majesty the Queen excepted. Your height is the only thing to recommend you. You may even aspire to a bank clerk, bearing him first a boy and then a girl, in that order." She wagged her finger then. "All these women bearing girls first thing! What in heaven's name are they thinking? They aren't, that's what."

My great thanks, Cousin Matilde, for your generous view on my future life.

March 7th

Today I canvassed nearly all of St. Crispian's. It was a ritual of my father's, beginning each stay at Lapis Lazuli with a survey of the neighbourhood, and I have continued the practice.

It is a glory to be in London again, and even better to be in St. Crispian's. It has always been the favourite neighbourhood of mine, settled so near Primrose Hill. Much of London's uncanny history is jostled together here. The fifteenth century church built over a Celtic burial mound. The remains of a Roman fort still standing watch at the top of Whereabouts Lane. The gallows, still intact sans rope, silently waiting in the middle of Traitors Road. If one reads the biographies of many a great—if slightly scandalous—Londoner, they often spent a few formative years here in the wonderful St. Crispian's.

Miraculously, St. Crispian's boasts a fair amount of *respectability* as well, due to both Sterling Street and Baron's Square. The Lady Trewartha lives here, as well as Lord and Lady Blankenship, General Braithwaite, and the Duke of Islington. I myself cannot boast personal acquaintance, as I am a stumble or two below their lofty class, but in a place like London, one always knows of the most important people living nearby. You can't help it. Gossip is as catching as the plague ever was.

Admittedly, there are some unusual things about the neighbourhood. The architecture in places could be called eccentric. The flora and fauna tend to grow at an astonishing rate. It must also be disclosed that there are some other *peculiarities* we tend to not discuss openly outside the neighbourhood. But truly, St. Crispian's is almost perfectly normal.

Almost.

Every shop front does have its signage either upside down or backward, considered a mark of good luck since the ascension of Charles the Second. I know not what to say except it seems to have worked. All the businesses on King Henry's Road do very well.

St. Crispian's is tucked snugly—and snugly is perhaps too generous a word—between Primrose Hill and Primrose Hill. Meaning, it consists of four streets with various appendages, and a square, set down right in the middle of the neighbourhood of Primrose Hill. A state inside of a state—rather like the Vatican. The three main roads are as follows: Traitors Road, towards the west; my own Whereabouts Lane on the east; and in the middle, Sterling Street, very properly leading up to Baron's Square. These three are all traversed by the Diagonal, and undergirded by King Henry's Road.

As previously mentioned, Sterling Street and Baron's Square are *reputable.* Very. The houses are all of uniform design, each painted white, with roses flanking the stairs leading up to each perfectly painted green door. However predictable, I enjoy my walks there.

Whereabouts Lane, my own piece of St. Crispian's, is nothing of the white and green, rose-adorned glory. Rather, it is a hodgepodge of brick and stone, all grey or cream or reddish-brown, with each of the doors painted a slightly different colour. It has always been this way. Every ten years or so, the residents of Whereabouts Lane invite a painter (usually French) to come and select the colour palette for the doors and shutters, with the exception that Lapis Lazuli's doors remain, well, Lapis Lazuli—brilliant blue that it is. In the mid-1870s, the artist Edouard Louis Dubufe was invited to select Whereabouts' palette. Now that we're in 1883, there is again talk of a fresh scheme. I only know because Cousin Archibald wrote of the debate to Cousin Matilde. Some are pushing for it to happen soon. Translation: Mr. Morrow is tired of his front door being pink.

On the west of St. Crispian's, Traitors Road is all grey limestone brought down from Scotland. It hosts gallows, as previously mentioned, and is popular with the London bachelors and several young gentlemen who see it as a great adventure. (Byron once held a drunken duel in the middle of the road. Thrilling to young males everywhere.) The current residents pride themselves on the most unusual lamps outside their doors, and it is a bit of a game among the younger sets in London to walk the street in the gloaming before full dark to see the lamps in their glory. My favourite is a fox with a bird in his mouth, the bird being the light, only fitted with wings.

While respectable Sterling Street glides straight up the hill, ending in the beautiful Baron's Square, both Traitors Road and Whereabouts Lane unravel into a few random side streets. These tucks give them a very irregular feel, and it is almost impossible for carriages to turn around.

The Diagonal cuts from upper Traitors to lower Whereabouts, politely crossing Sterling on its way.

All this considered, the best part of St. Crispian's is the tall house with a blue door that resides in the quirk of Whereabouts Lane.

Home.

Maxwell was always entertained with my stories of St. Crispian's. He said he would come to London when I did and take up rooms on Traitors Road.

"Certainly not. You would be a guest at Lapis Lazuli House," I'd insisted.

Part of me still expects to see him walk through the front door.

March 8th

I am going to have to deal with my garret. A discouraging reality. A rigid practice in avoidance might be endurable for the present, while sleeping on the narrow bed stuffed between odd bits of furniture, my few belongings strewn about, but the dust and cobwebs are demanding attention. Perhaps tomorrow.

Agnes has told me something of interest—and thus the promising side of her unpromising nature peeks through a window. Apparently, The Roman is spending his nights on Traitors Road.

The Roman is a centurion that guards St. Crispian's. A ghost, in other words. Not that I've seen him myself, but nearly everyone has a story—Mrs. Bailey, Mr. Ford, even the esteemed bachelor Plithco Wright, whose garden claims as prize a portion of the wall.

According to local lore, it was he—The Roman, not Mr. Wright—who very first ordered the wall built that separates Whereabouts from Magi Street. The wall is only partial ruins now, but everyone speaks as if it's in full glory. The Roman never wanders too far from his beloved ruins, which is why an appearance on Traitors is worth a mention.

They say The Roman speaks proper English because seventy years ago a professor of Latin took up the job. I, sadly, cannot personally confirm the fact.

As close as we are to Primrose Hill and Regent's Park, we in St. Crispian's boast a small garden of our own. It is found through a gate—a stone passage in reality, with two benches set inside its elongated arch—that rests on the top end of Whereabouts. There is a small lawn, a corner of trees, and some beautiful brick walls on three sides of the park. The fourth is completed by the remains of the Roman wall. We call the garden Jacob's Well. No one seems to remember why.

I asked Agnes this morning if The Roman has been seen at Jacob's Well, a favourite haunt for him in the past. She laughed at me as if I'd told her I was a frog.

"Of course not, Miss Lion. Where would the monks practice?"

I blinked. "The monks?"

"For the last two months, the monks from St. Benedict's have let Jacob's Well from midnight to dawn," Agnes answered.

"Is that the singing I heard last night? I'd supposed I was dreaming."

She looked at me like I was daft. "Of course. What else would it be?"

What else, indeed?

March 9th

I walked longingly past The Dalliance today, St. Crispian's Bookshop. I did not go in. There are realities we must face, an empty purse being one of them. I did pause before the front window and read the placard, which—being read backward—states that they sell books of the 'New, Slightly Used, & Abominably Treated Yet Resurrected Variety'.

I adore this shop, but the price for even a resurrected book can be quite steep. And the bookseller, Mr. Graves, has not looked directly at me since I sold my father's collection to another bookseller to finance my education. But I was at my aunt's house in the country. She was not going to let a thirteen-year-old girl take hundreds of books by train to satisfy Mr. Graves.

Alas.

Upon returning home, I sent the following to my cousin,

Arabella,

Spring has come. This change in the weather will do me good, I think. I look forward to seeing you next month in London.

Yours ever,
Emma

A few hours later I received this,

Emma,

Make the most of your early Spring. London is due for a storm. I expect rain, but the thought is not insupportable if one is prepared. The rain will not deter dear Mama, as she has many delights planned for both of us. Surely all the sun we will need. Prepare yourself for what awaits.

Always,
Arabella

We are usually not so concerned with weather, but at Christmastide Arabella and I agreed upon a scheme. I would go as far as to say we concocted it, for going against Aunt Eugenia always feels like toying with a witching hour. The scheme goes as follows: I would arrive in London the beginning of March, while Aunt Eugenia would be given the impression I was to arrive at the beginning of April, buying—or rather stealing—an entire month for me to settle in before the edicts begin rolling down from Spencer House.

But what of the lack of a postmark? This thing is easily explained: I sent the note by way of Toff—a local boy earning money for school by running messages for the residents of St. Crispian's—and placed said note in an old envelope I'd already sent Arabella, bearing postmarks from Bournemouth.

Clandestine, indeed.

Arabella and I have now stolen the March on Aunt Eugenia to the tune of a solid month, and neither of us feels any remorse. When I began to fret we might be found out, Arabella looked at me with her forget-me-not blue eyes and said, "Emma, screw your courage to the sticking place."

Quoting Lady Macbeth is not, perhaps, a morally comforting thing, but it did the job with aplomb.

It's a relief. To have such crisp, clean days spread out before me. No Cousin Matilde to forbid my breathing. No Aunt Eugenia Spencer to order me about. And, as of yet, no Cousin Archibald to tempt me to violence.

March 10th

I had some urgent mending (meaning I split another seam on my brown jacket and ripped a rather enormous hole in my skirt while shifting furniture around the garret), so I took it down to the kitchen and talked with Agnes while she was chopping vegetables.

She's a skinny little thing, a freckled bird with straw-coloured hair. She was hired by Cousin Archibald as the housemaid six months ago, and soon after, when the cook quit, was given all kitchen responsibilities as well, with no increase in pay. How appalling, something I will remedy when I have the power.

"I don't mind it," Agnes said as she prattled away, the steady pace of my needle tricking her into thinking I was fellow help. "It's easy enough to make soups and bread and puddings, and as there are no formal meals, Master doesn't need much more than that. It's Parian who can complain like the dickens."

"Cousin Archibald does not need to be called Master, Agnes. Calling him Mr. Flat is adequate. As for Parian, if he can find an equally comfortable situation elsewhere, he is welcome to try."

She giggled.

Agnes is from the southern border of Scotland, but her mother, intending for her to go into service for a wealthy English family, made her prune her wild accent until it was 'proper'.

And she ended up at Lapis Lazuli. Poor girl.

At one point she said, "You have such a lovely voice, Miss Lion."

I snorted, a noise entirely beyond my control, and laughed. "Do I?"

"It's different—it's a purplish grey, like dusk. A bit scratchy."

"You make me sound like a thistle," I answered.

"My mother used to tell me that a girl with a voice like yours could have any man she chooses."

I'm certain her mother is a wise woman, but that's the most ridiculous thing I'd ever heard.

I told her so.

She giggled again, the freckles on her face brightening above her flush of amusement. "My mother has an opinion about everything, Miss Lion."

I'm certain she does.

March 11th

Rain, dismal enough to be cosy.

March 12th

A report of battle must be passionless, stern. That is what I wish to manage today—the stiff, fact-relaying tone of a war correspondent, for I do not want emotion to muddy it up.

The plain facts are these: I was promised an allowance. To be paid to myself out of the living that goes with this house—mine by technical right. Said allowance has yet to be delivered. Cousin Archibald seems reluctant to address the issue. Meaning, I have knocked on his study door every time he's returned home and asked about it, and he has refused to answer.

Truthfully, I am also owed a salary for three years of working as a companion to Matilde. I'd enquired after my payment when the situation had first been proposed. Being fresh out of school, it was suggested I forgo drawing on my salary—instead, letting it build up into a Tidy Sum in the bank. Those were Archibald's exact words. Tidy Sum.

"My sister and I will save your salary for you so that when you come to live permanently in London, you will have a *Tidy Sum* to set you up."

"As well as an allowance from the living," I'd added.

"Yes, yes. As stipulated, you will receive the allowance promised. Given you will already have such a *Tidy Sum*, you will be a fortunate girl, indeed."

Fortunate? Three years as a companion to Cousin Matilde? Fortune could not in all good conscience be called upon.

Despite his eagerness, it sounded wise. Three years of salary would mean a degree more of security to start my independent years. But each time I have tried to engage Cousin Archibald in conversation, he does not open the door. Or acknowledge my existence.

In regard to finances that one does not possess but is owed, I believe in being cavalier as a general rule of thumb. Act for one's own good or be crushed by the uncertainties of the future, is the motto I live by. I admit that adopting that motto is somewhat daunting just now.

Cousin Archibald continues to stonewall me, my three years' pay is still a nebulous promise, and no allowance is forthcoming.

Knowing Archibald Flat as I do, I had little expectation that he would greet me with my owed salary, my allowance, and a paternal kiss on the cheek (thank goodness). However, one hopes the fiduciary allotment is forthcoming.

I could use the singular comfort of a Tidy Sum in my bank account.

Ah, there. I hear a commotion downstairs. Cousin Archibald must have returned. Perhaps I can ambush him before he can hide behind the lock of his study door.

March 13th

I was up late reading Book One from *Paradise Lost.* Once the hour turned from late to ghastly, I snuffed out the light and sat at the window, looking for The Roman.

He did not appear.

This morning I have only a headache to show for my great anthropological efforts. I asked Agnes, when she brought me my breakfast, if she has ever seen The Roman herself on Whereabouts Lane.

She has not.

Well.

Selected Notes From My Reading

* "*Confounded though immortal!*" found on line fifty-three. If that is not counted a lovely pairing of words, what is?

* I've been sitting at my window repeating this line for a quarter of an hour: "*From morn To noon he fell, from noon to dewy eve...*" From noon to dewy eve. I don't know if I've ever done anything from noon to dewy eve. Maybe I should try. Granted, this was a fall from Heaven, which is not likely to be as pleasant as a long read beside a window.

* "*...while overhead the Moon*
Sits arbitress, and nearer to the Earth
Wheels her pale course..."

March 14th

I found myself wakened in the early hours to a sound that haunted me at school.

The scurry.

The scrape.

The scratch.

Followed by an all too earthly squeak.

The garret has mice.

I weep.

March 15th

The last two days I have gone about situating myself in a manner which can only be described as Wild. It is the Ides of March, after all.

I began by moving all items, save the wardrobe and the bed, from the east room to the west room. Agnes's help was enlisted for the larger pieces of furniture. Parian was nowhere to be found.

Not long into the project, my middle-of-the-night suspicions were confirmed. There are indeed mice in the garret. Their droppings were underneath every dusty piece of furniture we moved. Which resulted in me fetching hot water and a bucket from Agnes.

"Do you need me to do that for you, Miss Lion?"

"No, no," I told her. "This is my battle, and you've a whole house to clean."

In truth, I wished to know it had been scrubbed to a severe level.

I scrubbed and scrubbed and scrubbed with hot water and lye. My hands are red and blistered, but every surface of these two rooms has been cleaned twice over.

Against his will, I ordered Parian out for some white paint.

"I'm not asking you to help me, Parian," I told him, when I found him in the drawing room with his feet quite *up*. "I am only asking you to use your feet for something other than what you're doing right now."

"You have yet to produce sufficient monetary inducement," came his reply.

"Both you and the paint can find inducement from your pay and the household accounts respectively," I informed him. "I may live in the garret, Parian, but I am the legal owner of this house, and when I am one and twenty—a blessed event which happens in January—I will no longer need Cousin Archibald to play guardian. My new-found authority may easily extend to the house purse, which pays your wage."

This vulgar reality was the trick. He sprang to his feet and informed me the house would be happy to supply the paint, and did I need brushes as well?

March 16th

Cousin Archibald is still sneaking in and out of the house like he's burgled something. While my imagination would enjoy the notion of him turning thief, the truth is he has avoided me since The Incident of The Scar.

Perhaps I should put a bell around each of my ankles so he can hear me coming, like a cat.

March 17th

Parian must have mixed my paint up with the milk delivery. It was soppy and thin, but I was determined. I have gone over the floor, walls, and the ceiling four times. The paint tins are dry, the brush in a state only for the rubbish, but my room is now...pleasant. Not perfect, but fresh. It feels like a cottage by the sea rather than a London garret. I say room in the singular because I only had enough paint for the east room. Even if I managed to convince Parian to repeat his charitable act and procure more paint, I don't have it in me to lift another brush.

March 18th

As I was negligent last Sunday, in the spirit of reformation I made my way up the Diagonal to where it meets Traitors Road and attended church—in the previously mentioned chapel originally built in the fifteenth century over a Celtic burial mound. It was refurbished in the seventeenth century. Scholars debate this—not the refurbishment, the burial mound. But St. Crispian's holds firm.

Our vicar is called Young Hawkes, although some of the gentlemen who rent rooms on Traitors Road call him "Hawkes the Fox" or "Mighty Nigel Hawkes"—appalling, entertaining, and wonderful—for Young Hawkes was at Eton and Cambridge with several of our disrespectful but affable single gentlemen, and is only seven and twenty years of age.

He came to St. Crispian's eight years ago to study under our old vicar, Father May. Father May spent three months introducing Young Hawkes, as he called him, to all those who dwelt in St. Crispian's, be they Anglican or not. After said three months, Young Hawkes was asked to give the sermon.

This particular Sabbath is burned into the collective memory of the neighbourhood, and I was lucky enough to share in the moment as it was June, and thus I was visiting Lapis Lazuli House with my parents.

Everyone was curious to hear what the young curate would have to say. He was a mismatch for the profession. His hair, never quite tidy. His face, rather too well-formed for a career in the church; and on that fateful day, his friends from Eton and Cambridge were filling up the back pews, silent but heckling just the same.

Young Hawkes stood and delivered the most tremendous introspection—and introspection it was, for instead of a dry sermon, he simply forgot the congregation and began an hour-long conversation with God.

He spoke of Grace, wrestled with it. His words part prayer, part soliloquy, and part an exploration of himself, his motives, and God's place in it all. We all sat enrapt.

I do not wish to give the impression that it was maudlin or over-indulgent. Indeed, it was his unassuming honesty that gave his words their strength. He seems to know just what to do with language. It hovers beside him, a fluid and mischievous thing, like Prospero's Ariel. And so Young Hawkes weaves spells with words and we sit entranced.

The emotion of this first sermon mounted and mounted until we were all sitting on the edge of our seats, leaning forward, breathing shallow breaths. And when Young Hawkes finished, there was silence in the chapel for the space of what felt like half an hour but was merely seconds. Then applause.

I have never heard such a clap in a church, and I doubt I ever will again.

Father May, observing it all, let the trespass of a slow smile cross his face, and the next morning he simply disappeared. The police were not informed as several witnesses saw Father May leaving the neighbourhood, cases packed, on his way to the docks where he would catch a boat to America.

Young Hawkes received a letter from the diocese that a more experienced man in the priesthood would be sent to replace Father May in due course. Eight years later, Young Hawkes is still our vicar, still goes by that name, and three Sundays of every month he gives a sermon.

A neighbour on Whereabouts Lane once said, "I can't afford tickets to the theatre on a regular basis, but no matter; we've got Hawkes. Did you hear how last month he quoted entire swathes of *Hamlet* from memory and sounded as good as any actor you'll find on stage?"

On the fourth Sunday of the month, worn out from three weeks of sermons, Young Hawkes simply stands at the pulpit and reads his favourite passages of scripture, along with the occasional poem. The last few years he's been favouring the Romantics. Hearing that man read is wonderful. Especially when the poem itself is less religious and more inclined towards the sentiments of the heart. Those he usually reads when a few of the elderly members of the congregation have nodded off.

We are all enamoured with this vicar of ours.

During the week he is a rare bird. Instinct tells one to leave him alone unless he introduces conversation first. It is not that he is a hermit, or narcissistic, or odd—he simply maintains an economy of interaction that is spare in its elegance.

While one does not tell Young Hawkes of their needs, somehow the widows are heard, the sick cheered, the lonely remembered, and the drunkards are… Well, I honestly don't know what he says to the drunkards, but I know he speaks to them a lot. He keeps rooms on Traitors Road, diagonally from the church and next to The Cleopatra, St. Crispian's public house.

I've never spoken with him myself, but three years ago when I was visiting Cousin Archibald, I passed Hawkes on Traitors Road, near his rooms. Upon seeing me, he closed his book—he always walks with a book—and bid me wait.

That was all.

He said, "Wait."

Then Young Hawkes disappeared into the door of the building where he lets his rooms. Wait I did, more than a little confused.

After several minutes, Hawkes came out and handed me a card. "Miss Lion," he said, and then he was gone. I blinked rapidly a few times as I watched him pass The Cleopatra then cross the road, towards the church. After he went inside, I looked down. On a cream card a single word was scrawled: *Imperterritus*. I flipped the card over, and embossed in gold was a beautiful lion. It was not docile, neither was it ferocious or violent, rather, it was undaunted. Which is what, I learned upon investigation, Imperterritus means in Latin.

Undaunted. Fearless.

I took the card home and have kept it ever since. Miraculously, as I was using it to bookmark Cousin Matilde's Bible, it survived The Great Burning of 1882.

I haven't shared the story with anyone. It is our secret, his and mine. We have not spoken since.

Young Hawkes looked much the same in church today. He spoke on biblical feasts, and as his eyes considered the congregation, I believe he noted my attendance and gave the subtlest nod of acknowledgement.

March 19th

Cousin Archibald finally found the courage to show his face. He still bears The Scar under his left eyebrow. When he came into my room—for I was not invited downstairs—he made certain to sit by the window, with just enough light falling upon his face so that it might be clearly seen. It was very Dutch Painter of him. I almost suggested we hold a séance and call up Vermeer.

Cousin Archibald is a firm believer in forgiving everyone their trespasses except me. Me he desires to burn in eternal torment.

Our conversation went like so:

"I see you found your way here," said he.

"Are you disappointed I did?" said I.

A pause.

"No. No, no, no. Indeed, not. Here you are. I suppose Matilde could not keep you forever," said he.

No, she could not, thought I.

"I'm not certain your sister is quite sane, Cousin Archibald," said I.

"Her last letter was perfectly sound. I felt moved by her words and was touched, really, at our kinship of blood manifesting itself in similitude of opinion."

At which point I frowned.

"That entire letter was a gross defamation of my character," said I.

I know this because I wrote out all her correspondence—one of my many duties—and posted it myself. Damned by my own hand.

"You do her abilities of perception a discredit," said he. "And her generosity towards you, as my heir, though you hold no blood relation to either of us, was unparalleled."

My teacup broke ~~from excessive force~~ somehow. I smiled, tea staining my gown, and answered, "Unparalleled, indeed."

He had the decency of looking away—making his lie easier for both of us—and stirred his tea, clinking the spoon against the cup whilst he looked about the room.

"I hope you find your lodgings to your taste," said he. Not rooms.

Lodgings. As if I had no claim on this house whatsoever. Or as if I were an outlandish American on the Western frontier, looking to stay at a questionable boarding house while I spent my days in the hills searching for gold. Which upon further reflection, sounds like a valid possibility if living in London does not suit.

"My rooms are quite charming. I shall be very happy here," said I, answering honestly.

He ran his fingers through his thin hair, the shine from his head transferring to his fingers, then reached for one of the scones Agnes had prepared for our tea. "Such it is, such it is," he said in consolation to my happiness. "If you'd prefer a room on the third floor…" said he.

"Near Parian?" exclaimed I. Heaven forbid. "I would rather avoid that small hell, Cousin."

He took great offence at my knowing the word hell—I do read my Bible—and left.

It was our most cordial conversation since The Scar, says I.

March 20th

I am satisfied with the state of my living quarters. Of course, one can hardly welcome an acquaintance into a garret, but the only people I foresee visiting are Arabella—who will laugh—and Mary—who will be delighted.

Today I have performed two acts of theft. The first was to sneak down into the rooms on the fourth floor and find a suitable carpet.

In a dusty bedroom I found a partially rolled-up Turkish carpet. It is beautiful, woven with the colour of sunset—not orange, not pink, but somewhere in between, with designs of green, turquoise, and warm purple. It is very big, and I first measured it with a stretch of ribbon, worried it would not fit my garret. But it did. It left me an excess of five inches all around the perimeter. After pulling Agnes aside and demanding a blood oath for her secrecy, we waited for both Cousin Archibald and Parian to leave the house, then we carried it up the stairs. It took a good deal of effort, but ascend the mount we did, and with floor, walls, and ceiling all painted white, it looks positively like a painting on the floor.

The second theft, which I don't suppose truly counts, was that I found a bookcase in the west room of the garret and have commandeered it for my own purposes. It is painted, of all colours, a beautiful green. I have no idea how it came to be such a colour, because I refuse to give Cousin Archibald the credit. Once Agnes and I moved it into place, we also selected two chairs, made more comfortable by an array of mismatched cushions, and placed a writing desk against the wall.

"It's...colourful," Agnes said.

I agreed. "My mother would have approved."

"Was she a Turk?"

I laughed. I couldn't help it.

"No, Agnes, she was not a Turk, but she loved bright colours, and always said it was her inheritance from her Portuguese mother."

"My mother would not approve of such bright colours," Agnes said.

"She doesn't even think people should be Portuguese."

"Oh dear," I answered.

After Agnes left, I sat on my bed and stared at the empty bookcase across the room. It represents regret and hope, this bookshelf. It is folly and experience.

Five empty shelves staring at you is a daunting thing, so I stood up, took *Paradise Lost* from the desk, and set it on the left side of the top shelf. Its brown leather spine has a stripe of deep red across it. Milton looks ready and willing and able to occupy the shelf alone until I can find him some companions. I appreciate his generosity. I truly do.

March 22nd

Seeing as how all of my personal journals were lost in The Great Burning of 1882, I make a record of my living relatives—with a few references to the dead:

On my mother's side, I have an aunt, Lady Eugenia Spencer. She is the only daughter of my grandfather's first wife. Seven years later, his first wife having died, my grandfather married my grandmother, a young woman from Portugal. My mother was born the following year. My mother and her sister were fond but not particularly close. My Aunt Eugenia, now a widow, has two children: my older cousin by five years, Damian, and my younger cousin by one year, Arabella.

It is on my father's side that I tie into Cousin Archibald—through marriage, a fact which relieves us both. My father is the son of an English gentleman and an Irish shopkeeper's daughter. He was raised in Ireland but maintained strong family connections in England despite being disinherited. His aunt, the first Emma M. Lion and an heiress in her own right, was given Lapis Lazuli House upon my father's disinheritance. She loved her older brother and therefore adored his Irish son, so even before she married, she named my father heir upon her death, to inherit both her London house and a living. She soon married a young man named Archibald Flat, and she and her new husband moved into Lapis Lazuli. As the Fates would have it, three weeks into their marriage she died of influenza. It was a shock to the entire family and, when her will was read, an even greater shock to her husband, Archibald. She had not made provision for him, leaving him only the books in the library.

My grandfather was generous, and considering my father was still quite young, agreed that Archibald be allowed to remain in the house and utilise the living until, upon Archibald's death, my father would enjoy his inheritance. Which is how my father came to make his own way in the world, whilst his living was enjoyed by Cousin Archibald. I don't begrudge the situation. It would be abhorrent to fling someone's spouse out into the world. But it's done all the time when it is a woman. I thought my grandfather and father extremely gracious, and Archibald less so.

One of the stipulations of the agreement was that my father visit once a year, usually in the month of June, to be a guest in Lapis Lazuli House—ahem, the house he owned. Knowing that he was living on my father's mercy, Cousin Archibald was willing to be somewhat hospitable. He may have been dour, but he was never too high-handed. The fact is that my father was the most charming, well-liked person anyone has ever met. Archibald dared not mistreat my father, for all of St. Crispian's loved him. No, Archibald only liked my mother, tolerated my father, and intolerated me.

It is when I inherited the house upon my father's death that Cousin Archibald's full resentment came to light. A new narrative was written between he and his older sister, the aforementioned Matilde. They insisted that Archibald felt he'd been given a raw hand. "He was tricked into love," Matilde said to me one afternoon, "forced to upkeep the house and family of a dead wife who had little enough consideration of him as to die young."

The absurdity.

Matilde said especially bitter things because Archibald refused to let her come and live with him at Lapis Lazuli, so she had to marry a man she disliked.

But even after my father's death, my yearly visit was honoured until The Incident nearly four years ago that resulted in The Scar. This is my first time back in the house since The Agreement of 1879, which we drew up while Cousin Archibald was still bleeding.

I do not plan to alter the current arrangements, but it is a comfort to know that I come into my majority next year and could dethrone him on every legal ground should he prove to be impossible.

How mercenary you sound, Emma M. Lion.

March 23rd

Today is Good Friday.

I lit a candle for Father, as it's the twenty-third, and then another for Good Friday because it felt like the thing to do. I sat by the window and watched the two reflections in the glass.

March 24th

I saw Maxwell today—or thought I did—standing on the street across from Regent's Park in a bit of late evening sun.

I was rattled, and the uncertainty forced my emotions into a wild place as I walked home.

It was so like him.

March 25th

Easter Sunday. I had expected a sermon that was more of a wrestle with God over the issue of mortality, but Young Hawkes simply read each scripture he felt referenced the Resurrection—symbolically, figuratively, or literally. Then he glanced up, gave his St. Crispian's congregants a long look, and said, "Amen."

I'm glad of it. I couldn't have borne a sermon today, even a beautiful one.

March 26th

Thinking of Maxwell again. Impossible not to. Not being able to see his grave has affected me more than I believed it would. I've never buried him, and so to part of me, he is very much alive.

It's happened several times, this seeing him, or thinking that I do. Along the streets of Bournemouth, or on the lane behind Matilde's house. Once at the graveyard near Barrows Edge after a Sunday service—that rattled me the most I suppose, seeing him standing there among the dead. But it wasn't him. The young man looked nothing like him, only he had a way of standing that I could have sworn was…

The initial moment is always the cruellest, the rush of recognition, and dare I say joy? Then the stranger turns and is just that, a stranger.

Sometimes a resembling figure will disappear around a corner before I can know for certain. Or simply was never there to begin with. I glance and there he is, but upon a second look, I am greeted with nothing but the space where a living, breathing young man ought to be, but isn't.

I wrote a letter to his brother, Evelyn, the month after I'd received the news of what had happened. It wasn't long, and I only asked one question.

How was it possible for someone to suddenly be lost to this world?

He never answered the question.

March 27th

Sent a note round to Mary telling her I'm in London.

To cheer myself up after a rather melancholy three days, I reread several of the letters she has sent me since we left school. I was laughing so, I had to throw open the window to breathe, my hands at my waist, tears on my face. It was such a blessed relief to laugh despite it all, and have Maxwell's ghost banished.

I think tomorrow will be better.

March 28th

Having regained a good deal of freedom—that might prove to be short-lived once Aunt Eugenia summons me and forces her will into my life—I am establishing my own blessed routine, namely that of taking two walks a day. One in the midmorning and one around sunset. These are both inconvenient times as far as socializing goes, which is perhaps why I've always been drawn to them. I enjoy the midmorning foray. I wake up, read, study, fuss over a few things, and then break out into the weather. It is good. Very good. But my true love is the evening walk, that last hour of daylight that has its way with sunlight, shadow, and soul.

That was the case this evening. The lamps were lit, light coming from the houses, and there walked I, alone, and not upset to be so.

March 30th

Mary called round today. What a breath of fresh air. She's droll, passionate, and a bit arch. Always has been. We were lucky enough to have roomed together at school—Fortitude, A Preparatory School for Girls—and have been the best of friends ever since.

Our room at school was a closet-sized affair, with beds that were too small for either of us and a wardrobe the size of a grandfather clock. Against school regulation we built a few clever shelves, undiscovered until the night Winnie Pepper Smith was caught strolling the grounds with a boy from Stoicism, A Preparatory School for Boys. Because of Winnie Pepper Smith's indiscretion, we were all routed from our beds and spanked with a paddle. At the age of fifteen. Mary and I each received an extra spank for having built clandestine shelves. The unjust thing was that in the uproar and punishment that followed, Winnie Pepper Smith herself escaped a paddle. She had been sent to the kitchen and been forgotten. Word went round the next day that the cook had fed her sweet biscuits with cream. It did not improve her standing in the savage nation that was Girls' Dormitory A.

As for Mary, she has been in London for the last year, living at a boarding house and working as a typist for the fascinating and radically new—and disapproved of by many—Edison Telephone Company of London, Ltd. She goes nowhere near the telephones themselves but is responsible for typing whatever her superior wishes to be typed. Yes, *typed*. Mary is one of the first typists in London. Her older brother gifted her with a typewriter—not as a kindness to her, but as a kindness to him. He knew she could find employment, and he could ignore her existence.

"It would have bored me to death, Emma," she told me, "had the pace of the work been any slower. But this new industry will take over the world in due time if the Post Office would only remove itself from our way."

"It's not surprising the Postmaster General is fighting tooth and nail against the industry," I said, sounding far more educated on the subject than I really am. "You can see how difficult it would be if everyone were able to say what usually must be sent through the post. That is giving the people tremendous power."

"There were plenty of people who didn't want the rabble to learn how to read or write, either, but where would the Postmaster be if the masses couldn't send letters?" Mary argued.

"There are still those who wish the rabble couldn't read and write."

We grinned at one another, for Fortitude, A Preparatory School for Girls is one such institution.

Mary works on Leadenhall Street for the telephone company during the day, and in the evening transcribes documents in her room for a professor who is endeavouring to write a comprehensive account of the recently deceased East India Company. As for where Mary lives, it is in a "clean and well-thought of" boarding house for young women located in Southwark.

"I am the blight on dear Miss Lamb's establishment," Mary confessed, swinging her spoon wildly about with her fingers while glancing out of the window.

"I'm surprised Miss Lamb lets you stay."

"Oh," Mary grinned, "she doesn't know I'm a blight yet."

Then she told me everything she's seen and done in London. I was duly impressed, as the young ladies at Miss Lamb's are allowed out only during work hours or when accompanied by an approved chaperone.

"Approved meaning...?" I led.

Mary rolled her eyes. "Approved meaning father, brother, or, after having gone through a rigid test of morality and conscience, a responsible male cousin. An aunt might hold sway if she were wealthy, but no others are allowed to lead Miss Lamb's poor virgin acolytes astray."

"But you've just finished telling me of the whole of London. How is it you've been escaping?" I asked.

Mary settled back in her chair and pointed at me with her teaspoon. "I, Emma Lion, have a cousin."

"You have no such thing, Mary Bairrage. I know, for fact, you've less interested family than I."

"Which is why I've hired one. Wait until you meet him—which you will, we've theatre tickets next month. Would you care to accompany us? It would be a good opportunity to introduce you to Miss Lamb, as things stand. My visiting you will be easier if I have her approval."

"I have only just finished being subjugated to the capricious morals of an old woman, Mary. You wouldn't dare put me through such an interview while the wound is still fresh."

"I would, Emma."

She promised me that getting approval from Miss Lamb would not take long, especially as her cousin would be present, and incomparably charming.

"What is this fictional cousin's name?" I asked, my tone voicing my dubious opinion of her latest venture.

"Jack."

"Oh dear."

Nothing good will come of a cousin named Jack, fictional or otherwise.

Near the end of Mary's visit, I asked, "Is your Miss Lamb related to Charles and Mary Lamb?"

"No." Mary shook her head. "She's not got one mad bone in her body. Unfortunately, my Miss Lamb is unquestionably sane."

"Alas," I replied.

"Alas, indeed."

Mary is a force of nature, to be sure.

March 31st

I sit here, staring at the empty green bookcase—save Milton, of course—ready to face the reality before me. Namely, my lack of education and my nonexistent library with which to educate myself—and that the blame for both of these bitter realities can be laid at my door.

It was difficult, when Father died, to see the forest for the trees. I was only thirteen and—with Mother suffering the final stages of consumption—on the cold edge of being an orphan. She followed him to the grave not long after, and there I was, on my own and responsible for my entire life. Granted, Aunt Eugenia was my guardian, but she was in Vienna with her husband on a diplomatic post and found my mother's death ill-timed. A thing with which I wholeheartedly agreed. Aunt Eugenia arranged for the vicar of my village to have me stay with a local family for the longest six months of my existence—Cousin Matilde notwithstanding—until she returned. Arabella was in school and Damian was, I believe, pretending to be at Cambridge. The pretence being he hired a young man to attend Cambridge in his stead, from the first day. An impressive feat that has gone undiscovered by everyone except Arabella and myself. The young man received a solid education and Damian, the degree. Thankfully, he doesn't do anything with it.

When Aunt Eugenia returned to England in the summer, I was brought to Spencer Court, their country home, and Arabella and I had a pleasant summer together. At the end of it, Aunt Eugenia announced she had found me a school.

"The best of schools," she insisted. "You will be well prepared for life."

I tried not to let the fact that its name was Miss Prim's School for Young Ladies quell my enthusiasm, but quell it did. The money my parents left me was just enough to cover a four-year tuition at Miss Prim's, only just. It felt like a wise investment as I was heir to Lapis Lazuli and its small living. But to my thirteen-year-old mind, the education I sought was not to be found at a school called Miss Prim's. I wanted Latin and Greek and all kinds of histories. I wanted science and theology and language and art. I did not wish to sew cushions all day. I did not wish to dance and sing.

When I voiced my concerns, Aunt frowned, widening her eyes at the ingrate I was surely proving to be, and with a huff informed me I might choose between Miss Prim's School for Young Ladies and an institution called Fortitude, A Preparatory School for Girls. Tuition at Fortitude was slightly higher than at Miss Prim's, and if I chose to attend there instead, I would need to sell my parents' belongings to make up the difference—the choice was left to me.

Arabella had the wisdom—cunning creature—to see I packed up one trunk of what I loved most to hide in the attic at Spencer Court. Among the few possessions I managed to keep was my mother's well-worn Bible—the portal through which I realised that there are stories in the Old Testament more fantastical than any of Grimms' tales—and my father's illustrated Shakespeare—meaning a volume of Shakespeare that my father himself illustrated, pasting the drawings inside the book. But one trunk was all we could manage. Everything else was my price to attend Fortitude, A Preparatory School for Girls.

My father had a well-loved, oft-read library. He pored over his books. He wrote in them. Scribbled on any open space with his racing thoughts. He wouldn't let me read too many of them.

"It isn't that you couldn't understand them, Emma," he said. "It is only that I want you to experience them when you're a little older, because the words will be richer for the mite of your own experience. You see? Give it another year, and you'll be ready to pilfer the treasures."

Of everything I had, it on with Father's books that hung the balance of my decision. I sat up all night staring at them. Opening the pages and marking his handwritten notes, drawings in every margin. His books were works of art. Oh how I wrestled. It was a night that took several years off my life, I am certain of it. I had an education in that library. A full, rich education.

But only by selling his library would I have enough to attend

Fortitude. When morning came, I made the best decision I felt I could. I do not blame myself. I had no true guidance. I went off the facts as I saw them. I wanted more than what most girls were being offered. I wanted to *learn* about this world. I wanted to leave school armed with a mind full of knowledge. And if I had to sacrifice my father's library so that I might live an entire life with the right start, I would do it.

Aunt Eugenia accepted my decision. Everything was sold, including the books.

I couldn't have known it then, but at Fortitude our education was ridiculously limited. We did not embroider, we mended. We were not prepared for a life of being gifted silver, we were taught to clean it. We girls were set to find jobs as housekeepers of the first order, governesses or nurses of the same quality, or become dutiful wives of an honest man—we were not deemed good enough for gentlemen. We were given Bible studies, but never able to read the book for ourselves, for there were texts considered inappropriate for us. We learned how to count money for household accounts. Cooking lessons were merely taking our turns in the kitchens peeling vegetables. We learned not how to attend a dinner party, but rather how to prepare the dining room for one.

Fiction of any sort was banned. Philosophy considered blasphemous. The mention of anything Greek or Roman branded us heathens. So you can see things were rather thin regarding the classics.

There were no music lessons.

We did learn *some* useful things. The horticulture mistress taught us more than how to harvest the virtuous vegetable; she smuggled flower seeds into the greenhouse. And where the headmistress usually read from Leviticus, Miss Charlotte—charged with our evening readings—would recite Isaiah.

Each day, swathes of time were given over to silent contemplation.

My quest for knowledge was starved.

I am not wholly ignorant. Spencer Court had a well-stocked library, and I've made it a habit to read any newspaper I see. But there is a great difference between knowing that Archimedes played a significant role in geometry and understanding how to execute his equations.

Last year, while in Bournemouth, I met a young woman who had just completed her education at Miss Prim's. She could read Latin, was fluent in history, art, science, could sing like a songbird, and was a picture of health, having spent enough time outside to ensure strong lungs. When she shared a charming anecdote from her Egyptian history class, I turned rather green with envy.

But I refuse to blame myself for my choice.

I could not have known.

This refusal to blame myself does not mean I don't feel absolutely ill when I think of my father's books and to know I could have had both: a solid foundation of knowledge and an entire bookshelf filled with my father's observations.

Why does life give such a decision to a girl of only thirteen?

April 1st

I have been summoned.

My vision of the morning included a solitary walk in Hyde Park, so I do not welcome being sent for—but when Lady Eugenia Spencer summons, one prepares.

I now consider my wardrobe and record a precise report of my circumstances, however melancholy the exercise. I can either wear the grey dress or the brown, which, in certain light, I can almost believe to be a faded purple. Those are the only two dresses I have to my name. Cousin Matilde, responsible for my clothing the last three years, has dressed me in a perpetual state of half-mourning. Or brown. Which, to the sensitive soul, is the same thing. She does not believe in colour on, and I quote, "An insufficiently funded young woman." As for my coats, they are of equal number. Two. A very stiff and cheaply made black—each time I wear it, I feel like an undertaker. And a brown—worn through and patched on both elbows. I patched them myself, choosing from the scrap bin a shocking green Matilde did not care for but could not prevent, for I mended my coat while she was asleep. Despite the coat being the colour of mud, it fits me perfectly. And the lining, while also brown, has a slight hint of flowers. When Matilde saw the demure floral, the following exchange took place:

"Flowers inside the brown coat of a poor girl is immoral," said she.

"Oh, Cousin Matilde! Did you say this brown coat makes me look immortal? Why, what a fine compliment. I shall leave you now and write it in my journal."

"What? What? I said immoral, not immortal, you daft child!" said she.

"What? What?" croaked I in return.

The croaking, I believe, was my undoing. After I'd been sent to the butchers, I'd returned to find Matilde in the middle of The Great Burning of 1882. Every journal, letter, every word I'd written, even the diary I'd kept as a child—ash. My own Alexandria.

It was hateful of her to have done. And I swore in that moment I would never return to that house once I was freed from my indentured servitude.

I digress.

As shabby and worn as it is, I believe I must choose the brown. It usually brings me good luck. And Lady Eugenia cannot abide a frayed sleeve. She might resolve to correct the blight with her own deep pocket book.

Later

Lady Eugenia Spencer is a wonder of this world. She is her own Parthenon. When I arrived at Spencer House, I was ushered in to the First drawing room—a good sign. She relegates society by which drawing room she will receive them in. Many are received into the Second; not considered a slight, but certainly a sign of limited esteem. The dreaded reception in the Third drawing room is whispered of among the London Elite, for the Third is reserved only for those Lady Eugenia wishes to see on the scaffold someday. Even as far as Bournemouth, I heard a rumour that only two months ago Lord Sharp called, with the intent to visit Her Ladyship and my cousin, Arabella Goddess Divine. Lord Sharp is a scoundrel of the first order and every order after. Simply, he is a man with no morals and excellent taste in just about everything else. He was received in the Third drawing room. A greater man would have cowered. Lord Sharp, a lesser man than most, promulgated the rumour himself.

Reining my wandering, gossip-mongering thoughts, I return to the First drawing room, into which I was received.

Aunt Eugenia was sitting on the sofa, leaning against several pillows covered in feathers, as if a flock of geese had expired on her sofa. Still, there was an elegance to the pseudo-taxidermy. The room glowed with expensive fabrics, the curtains hung perfectly, and the windows were open to the garden.

"You always look ill, Emma. I can't understand why you insist upon it."

"I believe it is a requirement, now that I am an orphan who lives in a garret, Aunt," I replied.

"The garret? Hmm. How is the dear old fool?"

"Do you refer to Lapis Lazuli House or my cousin?"

"Upon you mentioning a distinction, I admit to never having considered them separate entities. When he dies, you will have to call an exorcist to separate the two."

I laughed.

Tea was served, and I prepared myself for a barrage of questions. The wisest strategy when dealing with Aunt Eugenia is one of limited information. Keep your answers brief, tidy, and without too many loose strings she can pull at.

"How was your journey to London?" she asked.

"The trains ran on time."

"Did Matilde's new companion seem a correct sort of person?"

"As correct as a girl that age can manage to be, but I expect a bitter end."

"Hmm. Do you realise, Emma, how unflattering your hair is, arranged like so?"

"No, Aunt. Thank you for enlightening me."

I then ventured a question of my own. "Is my cousin Damian returned from the Continent?"

"Do not mention that canker to me." Long pause for effect. "No, Damian is not returned. He's in Greece."

"Lovely."

"Not lovely."

I shrugged, and withheld my observation that opinion is often a subjective beast.

Arabella was not home, having gone out in the company of Lord Brookstone, the glamorous Lady Brookstone, and their two mischievous and thoroughly enjoyable sons, Phineas and Oliver. I know them better than one would expect from one of my station—lowly, as Cousin Archibald, Cousin Matilde, and Lady Eugenia remind me often—for I spent a few weeks every summer in their company. Once they realised that I wasn't being pushed on them as a potential bride—and never would be due to my aforementioned status—I lost the cumbersome suspicion of being a wealthy & titled female seeking a wealthy & titled male, and I was fully accepted into their tribe. Through sacred ritual. We have been veritable chums since, exchanging the occasional letter. Arabella, despite the cross of being both wealthy, titled, and very marriageable, has also been accepted into the circle of their affection. It is no surprise with her hair of angel gold, resting like a crown above her fair skin and blue eyes—well, few young men can encounter a goddess and not reserve a place for her in their hearts. Even the unconquerable Phineas and Oliver Brookstone.

And I, being interrogated in the First drawing room, sorely missed Arabella Goddess Divine.

"I invited you here when Arabella would be absent," Aunt Eugenia said, divining my thoughts. "I wished to speak with you frankly, with no interference of an affectionate heart. You and I have Blood; that is more than enough for loyalty. As Arabella is affectionate towards you, her only cousin, she has no place in this conversation."

"I would not have expected anything less, Aunt. You do have the shade of Machiavelli following you about most days," I replied.

She sniffed, trying to decide what she thought of what I'd just said. Insult or compliment? I watched the decision hang in the balance, but then her right eye narrowed. Good, I thought. Insult. She's much more tolerable in such conditions. When slighted, Aunt Eugenia blooms.

"You should watch your tongue, Niece. I'm of half a mind to call the nuns to cut it out."

"Really, Aunt, nuns don't cut out tongues—not even of the youngest postulants."

"Oh, you are a Catholic now?"

"No, Aunt. But neither are you."

She sniffed. "This world depresses me. I thought we were living in an age of ideals. If the Catholics aren't cutting out tongues, who do we have left to rely on?"

"Perhaps the Welsh can pick up the practice?"

Aunt Eugenia squinted both her eyes at me. Her maternal great-grandmother was Welsh, and she doesn't like it mentioned.

Clearing her throat, Aunt Eugenia sat up straight. "I have decided, Emma, that this Season is to be The Season before *The* Season."

"*The* Season for selecting a potential husband, you mean?"

"Of course. I intend to be in my best form and secure several men of my liking to choose from."

Unable to help myself, I asked, "Is Arabella getting a stepfather?"

"Stepfather, indeed. Husband, more like it."

When my crooked smile came as answer, she glowered. "Tongue, girl. Remember the nuns."

"Yes, Aunt."

And then began the war council.

"One does not approach The Season with laxity, nor should one underestimate the importance of timing. Arabella will dazzle. I want several hearts on a plate before I'm satisfied. Once the man is selected, I will do what is necessary to ensure he proposes in the middle of next Season."

"Which would be *The* Season, Aunt."

"Of course."

I brought my teacup up to my lips. "So, This Season, is merely This Season. Or rather The Season, no italics."

"Did you capitalize the word This in your mind?" she asked shrewdly.

"I did. Capital T and capital S."

Lady Eugenia nodded her head approvingly. She believes one ought always to capitalize the essentials.

With the groundwork set, Lady Eugenia informed me that I was not to be seen with them during the month of April. "You may write to Arabella, of course, but then it is in May that your soul becomes mine."

I believe I choked. "Pardon?"

"You are to be the Foil, the Cousin, the *Spy*."

"The spy?"

"No. The *Spy*."

"Capital S?"

"Of course," she snapped. "With italics. This is important, Emma. There's no sense in dealing in improper nouns without emphasis."

"No." And I shook my head once to punctuate.

She stirred her tea and raised her eyebrows. "As I was saying, I will summon you in May. In the interim, I expect you to see yourself properly clothed. You look like a rag woman."

"I've not yet been given my allowance, Aunt. Until I do, my funds are nonexistent."

"No, no. Your allowance wouldn't cover you with a fig leaf. You will go to Madame Tasset on my charge. I may not have Affection, but there is Blood. And you are to be the Foil, you see."

"Oh, yes," I answered.

"Here is a card. You have an appointment set for Tuesday next. Choose whatever you like that will complement these colours." And she handed me a small box filled with snippets of fabric.

"Arabella's wardrobe, I presume?"

"Madame Tasset is The Best. Arabella is to be a picture. And you…"

"The complementary but unobtrusive picture frame."

A most pleased look crossed her face. "Indeed, Emma."

"I will do whatever I can in good conscience."

Lady Eugenia's right eye twitched above her smile. "Conscience has nothing to do with it. Necessity and Duty, rather. I am aware that your cousin, Matilde, arranged a chaperone for you, but there is no need to bring her with you to any events you attend with me. I will be chaperone enough for anything of import. You may use her for all your secondhand needs."

I opened my mouth to say, "Well, Cousin Matilde arranged for no such person," but something—be it fate, or an angel of deliverance, or my own judgement—closed my mouth before I could set the record straight. I simply smiled and allowed the misunderstanding to remain. That is what I believe Young Hawkes would call a sin of omission. A dishonesty brought about by neglect. I admit to having a full knowledge of the deed.

It took me a moment to realise that Lady Eugenia was still speaking. "…as you will be preparing for any event of note with Arabella, I will have a maid ready to attend to your needs. Now, away with you."

And thus ended the visit.

April 2nd

My first thought as I woke this morning, lying on my back and watching the light touching the walls through the windows, was this: Lady Eugenia Spencer assumes I have a chaperone.

Therefore, Aunt Eugenia Spencer did not arrange for me to have a chaperone when not in her company.

Therefore, Aunt Eugenia Spencer will never know I do not have a chaperone when not in her company.

It's all the luck of a falling star.

I took an early walk to consider my blessed fate. I am a responsible young woman. I am not foolish, nor ignorant. Most events will be under the chaperonage of my aunt, and when needed, I shall ask my friend Saffronia March to accompany me. She will be chaperone enough. Her last letter came from Venice, and I understand there she will remain until June, which only sets me a few months to manage on my own whims.

I look forward to seeing Miss March. She's a rare breed, an artist who actually sells her work. She is independent, intelligent, unafraid to speak her mind, and thirty-six years of age—which qualifies her not only to chaperone, but to move about as freely as a widow, only without the bother of having to outlive a husband. We became friends when I was young because she would come to Lapis Lazuli with her work and ask my father to speak brutally and honestly. He did. Miss March has told me in the years since that his critiques were what propelled her talents forward. We've been close since his death, mostly through letters, and have grand plans now that we are both to be permanent denizens of St. Crispian's. She lives further up the lane in a home with a studio and a view of our small park, Jacob's Well.

I don't suppose Aunt Eugenia will approve of Miss March, but I am old enough to wield a little power of my own. Even the Prince of Wales has purchased one of Saffronia March's Italian scenes. Who can argue with such esteem?

April 3rd

Sunshine, brilliant and inviting. The weather outside is quite nice as well. I walked up Sterling Street and around Baron's Square in the late afternoon, admiring the white pillars and wrought iron fences that guard the sleepy spring rose shrubs. The daffodils are waning, but there were some tulips.

I continued my sojourn into *Paradise Lost.* It certainly takes a long while for Lucifer to be cast down to the earth. My Great Sorrow is that I cannot scribble this copy up as it isn't mine.

For most, this would not prove to be any sort of problem. For Emma M. Lion, it is.

Alas.

The Reason Being I am doubly cursed. My tongue is quick while my reading is moderate, tempered, erring on the more laborious of paces.

April 4th

Most times what is amusing in my head is only that, in my head alone. This point was proved once again, only this afternoon.

Cousin Archibald invited me down to tea in the drawing room. I did not go expecting an olive branch, but thought that perhaps we would find some form of civility between us.

How wrong was I.

After he invited me to serve myself, Archibald's knee bouncing nervously, he informed me that Matilde was not going to be paying me the three-year salary owed.

Before my stammer could turn into verbal resistance, he lifted his hand as if he could stop my speech from the mere waving of an appendage.

"When you left Bournemouth, her best silver disappeared. She says she will pay you the salary once you return the silver," said he.

"But, Cousin, I haven't got the silver. I didn't *take* the silver," insisted I.

"We both know your propensity for bending the truth," whined he.

"That is a gross lie," said I.

"And what about the last cherry turnover?" said he, lifting a puritan eyebrow. "You have confessed thievery before. Why should you be believed now? The silver is gone and so are you. You will not be paid until it is found."

He had me. I did lie. Two years ago I had eaten the last cherry turnover, and when Matilde discovered the pantry bare, in a moment of panic, I claimed ignorance. The next morning I confessed, feeling it a great show of personal honour.

More fool me. She's used it against me ever since.

"Cousin Archibald, I did not take a single piece of silver, and I demand to be paid my rightful salary. You must believe me!"

"I choose to trust the words of my sister, now nearly ninety years of age, over that of a penniless girl of questionable morals," said he. Sneering.

I stared at the man. Stared without blinking, my mouth sealed in a flat line, my mind revolving around the extraordinary accusation. Penniless, says the man who is sustained by Lapis Lazuli House.

"This world is full of thieves," added he in that moment, "and I will not be taken in. And Matilde assures me you are among the very worst."

This shook me loose, and I bitterly threw a line of Milton at his face. "So spake the apostate Angel."

It was, looking back, a poor choice of words.

"What? What-what?!" shouted he. "Are you comparing me to that infernal fiend of the fiery pit?"

Apparently Cousin Archibald has also studied Milton.

I flung up a hand in defence, my other hand keeping my tea appropriately balanced. "No, Cousin Archibald, I am not. I simply cannot understand how you will not give me my allowance and now are refusing to see my salary paid," said I.

"Out!" And he took my cup and saucer right out of my hand, set it on the sideboard, and then gripped my arm until I was forced out of my chair. While escorting me from the room, he swatted me on the posterior as if I were a child. I lie not.

Quoth Milton, we were "in dubious battle on the plains of Heaven."

All in all, we have had teas which have ended worse.

April 5th

Upon returning from my morning walk I found my bookshelf empty. Completely. Milton had fled, or been kidnapped. I marched down to the kitchen to press Agnes into revealing the truth.

"He just went up and took it, Miss. Was nothing I could do. Then he went back to the library and locked the door."

"I am reading *Paradise Lost*! How could he take it? It was discarded in the attic. The thief!"

"That's what he said you were, Miss. Something about silver and Milton and a cherry turnover. He was raging and pounding, and when his morning robe ripped on a nail in the garret, he began cursing. I was too afraid to…" Then she paused, as if there was anything she could have done.

"I have had enough," I declared through set teeth. To the second floor I went, pounding on the door of the library until he opened it just enough for me to spy the stolen volume in his hand.

"I was reading that."

"The book is mine, and no ingrate will degrade the text."

"Ingrate? You live here only for my father's generosity! I want my three years' pay, and my promised allowance," demanded I. "Then I can buy my own Milton!"

"Don't be vulgar," said he, before slamming the door in my face.

Well!

The true vulgarity is that while my great-aunt did not leave Lapis Lazuli for Cousin Archibald, she did bequeath him all the books in the library.

I am beginning to suspect it was because she knew him to be a fool and hoped to provide remedy.

At this moment, it feels most unjust.

April 6th

This morning, after a restless night, I donned my coat and hat and very unfashionably walked to Bond Street, the tin of Arabella's dress scraps under my arm, hoping my appointment would distract me from my woes. I was admitted without delay—less, I surmise, as a sign of respect for my aunt, and more that I might not embarrass the establishment. It is a blessed relief they don't know about my great burgling past; else they might not have served me at all.

One cherry tart. One, for my sins. I would wager Lapis Lazuli House that Matilde sold her own silver and pinned the blame on the orphan known as myself.

I digress.

After being ushered into a dressing room, Madame Tasset came to attend me. She ordered I remove my clothes.

"Your aunt has given me *carte blanche*."

"In that case, Madame Tasset, we would both profit from a large order," I said, thinking of my pending poverty.

A true professional, she gave no reaction to my crude suggestion, but the light in her eyes glowed with profit, and I shamelessly fanned the spark into a flame. "As I am to be *closely* associated with my aunt and cousin, I feel it imperative to take her at her word. No expense should be spared. We should see I have the very best quality. Something with not only beautiful form but endurance."

Madame Tasset drew in the side of her mouth and, with a Parisian tilt to her chin, considered me. "Very well, Mademoiselle, we will see that you are abundantly set in the first fashion, yet with a timeless line. This is good for you?"

Now it was my turn to tilt my chin. "Très bien."

Two hours later I left in a daze, feeling as hedonistic as ever. Admittedly, I have no great need to be set in the first or even the second fashion. I want clothing that will last, in any colour other than brown. One might question how I have the gall to squeeze every possible item of clothing out of my aunt's generous coffers? The answer to that is simple. My aunt was given the guardianship of my person until I reach my majority at twenty-one years of age—a blessed event to come this January. But Cousin Archibald was given fiscal guardianship of Lapis Lazuli House and its living until I reach that same majority. Therefore, my aunt shuttled most of my financial needs—such as clothing—to Cousin Archibald, with the reasoning that the living would cover said expenses. (As if Archibald Flat would ever sanction a tuppence towards my keep while he legally holds the reins.) Aunt Eugenia, therefore, has ignored my wardrobe needs with an admirable and robust determination. I have received one dress every other year, left over from Arabella's discarded and outmoded pieces. But she was always shorter than I, and the hems never let down quite in the way a hem ought. Then she grew into a tall willow, and still the hems were made a mess of. Thus my guilt is...actually, nonexistent. And if this is to be the last time my aunt is willing to aid me, I, at very least, will be clothed.

Madame Tasset will deliver the following:

Six sets of underclothes. All inclusive. Only the best fabrics.

Three morning dresses. One light blue. One soft pink. And the last, a light silver.

Four day dresses. One deep blue-green, that looks like an ocean occasionally brightened by the sun. One grey, a lovely yet sturdy grey. The third, a rich, deep muddy red one you might call "ox blood." The last? Green. Bottle green. Neither muted, nor demure, nor appropriate. But the colour of moss after several days of rain. When I picked it out, Madame Tasset was suspect. Yet, upon holding it up to my face, she let herself smile. "You may be right. Your eyes, your hair... I will make certain the quality of this can be seen, so no one will make the mistake of thinking it a folly."

Heaven forbid I wear anything considered to be a folly.

As for ball gowns, I have four. An enormous extravagance. One emerald, simple yet sophisticated, for card parties or routs. The next, a deep, night sky blue. "If you are to show off the sweet beauty of your cousin, this will suit. It will be elegant but not claim attention, and you will look very thoughtful and intelligent. Let us hope you are.

Unless you hope to marry soon. Then let us hope you are not. It takes a courageous man to marry a woman with a mind."

My laugh at her mention of marriage was, perhaps, too jaded for one of my age.

Madame Tasset was undecided on the colour of the last two gowns. She fussed with the fabrics from Arabella's dresses. She frowned. She sighed. She picked out unobtrusive bolts of silk but muttered something about refusing to dress me as a dowager.

"I am an artist. I will not compromise my standards." She brought in a bolt of gold satin and one of wine-red silk. "You will complement your cousin in these, but they will make an equal. Your aunt will be displeased, but I cannot create something unjustly subdued. Of these, I will make your other two ball gowns."

She said my order would be ready three weeks from today. Until then, I can walk the parks in the anonymity of my patched clothing.

April 7th

The mice persist. I spent most of the afternoon stuffing whatever holes I could find with pieces of an old silk morning robe Cousin Archibald had discarded. Perhaps the fact that he once wore the garment will be enough to deter the rodents from entering.

April 8th

The mice seem to have rallied against me.

There were droppings on my desk when I awoke this morning.

It was a deliberate taunt.

My day proceeded like so: I informed Cousin Archibald I intend to visit the bank to see about household accounts. His sneer was as impressive as ever.

Arabella then sent a note asking how I was getting on with my unprecedented freedom. I answered that all was well, too ashamed to admit I've gone from prince to pauper rather quickly.

Aunt Eugenia also sent a note, telling me she was to have cards made up in my name.

> *If your card can make you look important, it is possible we may find a man thinking you are. After Arabella is Settled, of course. Let me know if you prefer lavender and silver or cream and gold.*

She is so very fond of me.

I replied saying,

> *Cream and gold, Aunt. By any chance could you have a lion embossed on one side? It might aid in the Illusion of Importance.*

The word choice was particular. Could is a challenge. Would is a favour. One might easily guess which would call Lady Eugenia Spencer to arms.

April 9th

Last night I had a dream about Maxwell. We were walking along the river between the Spencer Court and Barrows Edge estates, and it was a hazy, warm summer day. The grasses were gold. The greens, a lazy dull of late summer. The sky almost cloudless. We didn't say much of anything, but I was aware of Maxwell's hand holding mine.

"We've not gone far," I finally said, lifting my free hand to block the sun as I gazed out over the lake.

"Too far now," he said. Then it wasn't Maxwell but old Ezra Sturgeon, holding the empty bridle for Maxwell's horse.

"They bolted on me," Ezra said. "I was left holding this here bridle. Horse is gone. Boy is gone, too."

"Did you see which way he went?" I asked. It was too warm now, my clothes were growing sticky and my lips chapped.

"Too far now," came the sound of Maxwell's voice.

Then I awoke.

I lay there in bed unable to move. It had felt so very real, the press of his hand in mine. As I rolled over, cold air canvassed my cheeks. Lifting my fingers to my face, I found I had been crying.

Unwilling to lose myself again in nothing days as I'd done after his death, I forced myself to loosely follow my routine. I washed, dressed, and reviewed the notes I'd written on Milton before Cousin Archibald stole him. Two lines struck the image of my dream.

> *Cease I to wander where the Muses haunt*
> *Clear spring, or shady grove, or sunny hill.*

I did not feel a good deal of comfort.

Afterward, I pounded on Archibald's bedroom door for the requisite quarter of an hour, demanding he pay me what I am owed, followed by a slow walk through St. Crispian's.

I thought about entering the church.

I was tempted to enter The Cleopatra.

I did neither, instead returning home, not much better for the wear.

April 11th

Arabella came for tea today.

"Phineas and Oliver Brookstone send their love," she said once we were settled. "But I'm afraid they've fled to the Continent."

"Why?" I asked, more than a little disappointed. "It's only just the start of the Season. I was counting on their company."

"Too many eligible young women, apparently. Oliver was afraid he would be married before Michaelmas, and we can't have that."

"No, I suppose not. What did their mother say?"

Arabella's slow smile graced her face. "My dear Emma, it was Lady Brookstone's idea."

Had we all such supportive mothers.

When Arabella left, Agnes came to clear away our tea things in a bit of a fuss.

"What has upset you, Agnes?"

"I found another of Mrs. Killoran's wigs in the kitchen, Miss Lion."

"Oh? Have we had one before?"

"Twice before. She's always so thrilled to have them returned because it means prattling away as if I don't have a kitchen to run and a house to clean. I've my work, Miss Lion! There's no time to return her wig every time it wanders over!"

"Can you take the wig to the bakery?"

"No, she's on The List."

I lifted a helpless hand. "The rules of The List are nonnegotiable." Then, seeing her downcast face, "What if I were to take it tomorrow while you bake cinnamon cake? How does that bargain strike?"

She blessed me in English and then Gaelic and promised to buy enough eggs for the cake.

April 12th

Visited Mrs. Killoran this morning. She was pleased to have her wig returned.

"Bless you. It's my favourite. I'd wondered where it had got itself to. Once I saw Edward Norriage wearing it. Tea? I have so much to tell you, Miss Lion."

And tell me she did.

When I escaped an hour later, I wandered home by way of the Diagonal and let myself into the kitchen through the back garden, returning to my garret with a piece of cinnamon cake and the intention of reading the notes I'd made on Milton. Then I realised that while I have written several journal entries in the past, explaining St. Crispian's Rules for Items Personal, or RIP as the young men on Traitors call it, those records are, alas, gone. (See The Great Burning of 1882.)

And so I record again St. Crispian's one quality that is not found anywhere else I've ever heard of. Yes, we have a Roman ghost, and backward signs, and other oddities, but anyone can have those. This…unusual attribute is one we prefer to keep to ourselves. There is even a committee that visits any newcomer who moves into the neighbourhood, and politely explains the phenomenon. The facts are these: Items tend to go astray in St. Crispian's. No, they are not stolen, nor forgotten. They…wander.

A hat, or a cushion, or a book, may suddenly appear in the house of a neighbour, or a stranger living on another street altogether. The nature of these wanderings are not personal, they simply are what they are. Utterly random. I've had a hat pin, an umbrella, and a shoe disappear, only to be returned to me—if they were labelled—or to the Reed and Rite—if they were not. We usually had one or two things go astray each visit when I was younger. The only item that was never returned was a toy yo-yo. I blame Stephen Wheelwright for trespassing the rules of RIP and keeping it, for I saw him with one just like mine, and when I eyed him, he ran.

It is a system of highest honour, and for centuries even the most untrustworthy figures in St. Crispian's have done their part in keeping personal belongings where they should be. The legend goes that once Lady Trewartha's mother lost her ruby tiara. It was later found by a scullery maid in a house on Sterling Street. The maid, poor as a wildflower, promptly returned the tiara.

As a result of such unusual realities, the denizens of St. Crispian's label everything they can with their name and their house number. My personal labels read: Emma M. Lion, WL, 27. The WL for Whereabouts, clearly. Not all items can be labelled. One does not wish to have a label on a stocking, or a pipe. For such things we have the Reed and Rite.

The Reed and Rite is a tea house and bakery, and a shop for basic necessities. It has two front doors, one down on the ground floor, leading to the tea and excellent bakes, and one up the stairs on the first floor, where one can purchase the kind of things you often need but forget to pick up. Paper, ink, hair pins, watch chains, pen cases, with a few unusual gifts coming from faraway places. It is artfully practical, with a few displays of the fantastic.

The proprietor, a man called Jape, was tired of his merchandise disappearing and reappearing in others' houses. The items were returned, but it was a great inconvenience. So, in a bid to make his life easier, he set up a series of shelves in a back room of the tea shop, called The Keep, where all the wandering items of the neighbourhood could be placed. Consequently, when someone came in for tea and mince pie, they could look through the shelves and tables to see if one of their missing items had been returned. According to the rules of the RIP Society, if you find a personal possession in the back room, you are to locate the entry in the register, which has the name of the person who found it. You then date your claim and take it home with you. You may also bring a found item that is labelled to the Reed and Rite if you truly don't have time to take it directly to its owner. Anything that has been unclaimed for more than a year goes into a box and is saved for the annual St. Crispian's Rummage Sale, all proceeds being donated to the St. Crispian's Theatrical Society. The system has worked like a dream, and the theatrical society, which hosts *Julius Caesar* every July, has a robust allowance for costumes.

This brings me to The List.

If someone's name is on The List, their labelled items are required to be returned directly. It is one of St. Crispian's laws. (Yes, we have a few.) No dropping it off at the Reed and Rite for convenience. The Reed and Rite also sends a detailed catalogue of every unlabelled item brought to the shop within a month's time to those on The List. If one were to identify a missing item, a claim would be made by messenger, and their possession would be returned. Simple. Elegant. Dignified.

My name is not on The List. One must pay a robust fee.

As nothing of mine has gone missing, I have not been to the Reed and Rite since my return, but I think often of taking some of the very little money I have and going for a pastry.

April 14th

Today I met Mary's fictional cousin, Jack.

We attended the National Gallery collection at Trafalgar Square, spending particular time in the Barry Rooms. I enjoyed myself and would have enjoyed myself more had I not been worried Cousin Jack was planning to steal a few pieces from the Turner collection.

As for Jack…

He is of a height with Mary and reminded me of a large cat. Not the domestic kind—all fat and bothered by the world—but rather a jungle cat, sleek and purring and dangerous.

His hair, light brown and combed back from his face, was long enough to look roguish. Eyes, not memorable in colour but memorable in how they seemed to sharpen everything around him. His smile came easily, but I could almost see the marionette strings pulling it onto his face.

I don't trust him at all.

I met them both outside of Mary's boarding house in Southwark, where I was put through the ordeal of impressing Miss Lamb as a fit companion for Mary. She thought I was a tolerable person but was in raptures over Cousin Jack. He was *charm* itself.

Having secured Miss Lamb's blessing, we began our walk to Trafalgar Square. This was where proper introductions were conducted. Mary grabbed my hand and pulled me up short, while Jack slowed his saunter, a sly line lurking beneath his pasted smile.

"Emma—" Mary turned to me and waved a hand at the handsome devil to her right, "meet Jack Hollingstell, my dear and fictional cousin."

"How convenient that you are so fictional, Mr. Hollingstell," I said.

"Call me Jack, please," he replied, holding out his hand. I shook it, and then he offered me a cigarette.

I admit, I laughed at him. There was nothing of the polite in it. I very clearly laughed AT him. "Oh dear. Look at you. A proper Confidence Man. Which theatre did she drag you out of, Mr. Hollingstell?"

"Oh, no theatre, Emma," Mary interceded. "Hollingstell is a *younger* son."

"As one tends to be," I replied, a touch coolly despite my crooked smile. "One would never doubt your story of neglected nobility."

"A much younger son, Miss Lion," Jack answered with a laugh.

"Why don't I believe you to be one at all?"

He grinned, and it was wicked enough for me to believe almost anything.

"Miss Lion, regardless of what you may or may not know about me, I am an excellent fictitious cousin and will serve your friend in every respectful way. Now," he held out both his arms, "it would be my pleasure to escort you ladies to the Gallery. Shall we?"

We went, and there was a good deal of laughter between the two of them.

I intend to ask Mary the next time she visits how much of her hard-earned salary slips into his silk trimmed pockets. One cannot buy talent like that cheaply.

April 15th

Yesterday I received a letter from Cousin Matilde. She holds her ground on the silver and will not send the money owed. I am, in a most furious manner, unsure of what to do. I worked in good faith that my wages were being held. It was a demeaning three years, endured only with the promise that I would be rewarded in the end. Isn't humility to be rewarded? Are not the meek to inherit the earth? Why in heaven's name did I submit myself to such degradation if not to have three years' salary waiting for me?

Tidy Sum indeed!

I go to the bank tomorrow to personally sort out the allowance Cousin Archibald is so slow to provide. As for my Tidy Sum, I shall have to think on how to loosen Matilde's miserly hand.

As today is the Sabbath, I attended service. Young Hawkes gave a short sermon—his friends from Cambridge too ill from a night of over-drinking to create much of a disturbance—but after the final hymn, I sat in the pew until the church had emptied, not trusting myself to face Cousin Archibald without causing harm. I was concentrating on the rose window when someone sat at the other end of my pew. Glancing over, I saw Young Hawkes. I couldn't help but smile; he's such a misfit for the work he is in. Somewhat distant expression, hair askew, handsome profile visible as he looked up at the windows, Hawkes appeared more suited to a billiard room. The thought crossed my mind that Mary might find him interesting. Whether his aloof nature would appreciate her is another matter.

"It was a day for short sermons, Miss Lion, do you not think?" And his cold blue eyes flicked over to mine, the shadows on his face no less articulated than the shadows of the stone.

"I do. An empty church is more to my liking just now."

"So you've returned to St. Crispian's."

"I have."

"For good?"

"God willing," I answered, more of a mutter than an answer.

"Did I ever tell you," and he let the words fly away, following them with his eyes into the rafters before continuing, "that your father gave me one of his paintings before he died?"

"He did?" Eyebrows knit, I looked fully towards him. It was rare for my father to give away a painting.

Hawkes nodded. "It was during my first year here, and his last visit to St. Crispian's."

"Which painting?"

Instead of answering, he stood and said, "Enjoy your Sabbath, Miss Lion. I'm glad you're returned home."

He then left the church empty and myself somewhat dumbfounded.

April 16th

I have just been to the bank. After which I have walked the whole of London and am now sitting on a bench at the top of Primrose Hill. I ought to cry as discreetly as possible. I've settled for raging.

THAT ABOMINABLE, UNGRATEFUL, CONNIVING, PATHETIC, CRUEL THIEF.

Cousin Archibald! Cousin Archibald has run the fortune of Lapis Lazuli House right into ruin! Without any regard for my future, he has spent significant amounts of money. But not in stocks or art or anything that might yield an investment or a price upon reselling. It's all gone towards clothes. That's right. His extensive wardrobe, most of which he's *never worn*. And the greatest bills paid his tailor? Those for his morning robes, a thing I've always considered such a jest. My kingdom for a morning robe.

I arrived at the bank and asked to see Mr. Penury, of Penury, Penury & Jones. After some explaining to his secretary that yes, I did have business with him despite being female, I was escorted into his office. Upon my telling Mr. Penury of who I was, he said, "Ah, yes. Miss Lion. The inheritor of Lapis Lazuli House."

"And whatever remains of my great-aunt's fortune," I supplied.

A strange expression marked his face, but I'd not thought much of it until he called to his secretary—the young man who had almost denied me the appointment—and asked for the file to be brought. When my paperwork was before him, Mr. Penury did not even have to look at it.

"I am afraid to tell you, Miss Lion, that the bulk of your great-aunt's fortune is gone."

"Well, yes, Mr. Penury. I knew that. But when the accounts were reviewed three years ago by my guardian and yourself, I was ensured a small living, but a living nonetheless, even in the unlikely event of my great uncle living to one hundred and fifty. I have no illusions of a grand amount. I simply wish to keep myself in London, in Lapis Lazuli House, and buy books. I have considered owning a cat, but I believe that expense won't put me out in the streets just yet." I smiled then, foolishly, ignorantly. Mr. Penury had the good grace to chuckle, but it was restrained. "A humble but lovely dream, Miss Lion."

My smile froze on my face from the way he said it.

"Is there something I should know, Mr. Penury?"

He cleared his throat.

"Three years ago, you were correct. Such a dream could be attained."

"But?" I said, my jaw tight, my tone as pleasant as I could possibly force it to be.

"But," he smiled sadly, "Mr. Archibald Flat has added to his personal wardrobe at a rather astonishing rate since then."

"His wardrobe?" I asked, uncertain if I'd heard correctly.

"He has been to his tailor almost weekly, ordering several sets of clothing—"

"To say nothing of the morning robes," I interrupted.

Mr. Penury gave a polite but strained laugh. "Indeed. I am afraid to say that there is now fewer than three hundred pounds in the accounts."

I gaped. "Three hundred pounds?"

"Possibly less, I'm afraid. With a few outstanding debts. Once those debts are called in, and if you live humbly and cover your taxes, you can live on the remaining money for another year."

"One year?"

"One year."

"Does Mr. Flat have any other accounts?"

"I cannot disclose—"

"Mr. Penury," I snapped, "I have spent the last three years as a personal companion to Mr. Flat's awful sister. He has not paid me a penny of my well-earned salary. It was to be given me when I arrived in London so that I might have something put by. But my inheritance was to be my livelihood! There were thousands of pounds. You told me not three years ago I could live quite comfortably."

At this point I was speaking fiercely and at a loss for breath.

"Miss Lion, I have warned him several times, but he would not stop.

He also gambled at Sandown Park."

"He hates horse racing!" I cried.

Finally, Mr. Penury got the look on his face which meant he was willing to tell me everything. "I believe it was a way to make the money go faster. He bet several times on horses with injury."

"But why!"

"Are we being frank, Miss Lion?"

"Dash it all, yes!"

He made no mark of my language. "I believe Mr. Flat dislikes you even more than horse racing."

"He did this on purpose?"

"I believe so."

The numb truth went through me, and I felt quite disconnected from myself. "And you let him? Without a word to me? To whom the accounts legally belong! He was only an appointed guardian until I was twenty-one."

Now Mr. Penury had the good grace to look abashed. "I tried to reason with him, and even wrote you several letters to which you never responded."

"I never received a single one."

"I sent them all to the address in Surrey Mr. Flat gave me."

At this point I laughed, but it was rather maniacal. "Surrey? I've been in Bournemouth!"

Mr. Penury's mustache twitched. "He has lied to us both."

"Quite abominably. And your due diligence lacks any backbone, to your discredit."

He could not argue with that.

"I am willing to testify, Miss Lion, that there has been gross negligence, and turn the accounts over to your keeping effective immediately."

Effective immediately was effectively too late.

We sat in silence for nearly a quarter of an hour, and then Mr. Penury said, "There is yet an option for regaining some financial security, Miss Lion. You have one asset he could not, by law, sell."

"No, Mr. Penury—"

"Hear me out," he insisted. "Lapis Lazuli House is not the grandest house, by any means, but it is well looked after, a good size, and St. Crispian's has its admirers. There is also the small flat attached to the house. You could sell for a good price in this market. With those funds you could either rent some comfortable rooms or buy a smaller house. A cottage in the country. If you kept no expenses and found work—"

"Mr. Penury, Lapis Lazuli is my home and my birthright."

"Well, Miss Lion, it has been sold for pottage, so you must realistically confront your situation. Your father had explained to me the unusual situation of allowing Mr. Flat to remain at Lapis Lazuli, and to manage the household. He said it was the man's only source of dignity. It was charitable, but not wise."

I clamped my jaw together and looked away. He released a weighted breath, one full of sympathy.

"Perhaps we can find a way for you to remain. The flat remains unrented, I believe? We might find a way yet."

We agreed to meet again next month, allowing both of us to consider the matter further.

I cannot countenance even the thought of Cousin Archibald. I know he dislikes me. I know he's not yet forgiven me for The Scar. But to deny me my entire future!

What a pig-headed, two-faced, guttersnipe thing to have done! He is despicable. He is cowardly! He ought to be forever, forever in prison! Let him be stoned on Whereabouts Lane! He thinks he has seen me at my worst? Ha! Fear, Archibald Flat! For Emma M. Lion is an avenging angel more terrible than you can imagine!

SCOUNDREL! ROTTEN VILLAIN!

Later

The above ink blot is a direct result of my temper. It has cooled enough for me to see that wringing Archibald Flat's neck would be disastrous for my own future happiness. Prison would give me even less choice than I have now, however tempting.

That filthy blackguard.

He was leaving Lapis Lazuli House just as I was climbing the stairs. I could tell from his face that he recognised his error in judgement—meaning when he chose to leave the house, not having ill-spent all my money—but behind the pride there was something else. Embarrassment, perhaps? A shadow of shame? And both of us knowing what had been done.

"Hello, Archibald," said I, my voice as cold as any crypt.

He nodded and ran a hand over his greasy head.

"You and I have some business to discuss," said I. "I warn you now that due to my authority, you may no longer draw any funds from the bank. You will have to apply to myself for any personal or household expenditures. Now, I expect to sit down with you to discuss what has happened. You will be in attendance, dancing every polite grace upon me, or I will see you in the street, so help me."

This greeting seemed to do the trick.

"Of course."

"Bring the record of any outstanding debts you owe." And I swept past him.

I attempted to send a note round to Arabella. I could not.

I attempted the same for Mary but failed again. No, it was shame and stupidity so acute I could not share it. Not yet. Instead, I wrote to someone with no current opinion on the matter.

Maxwell,

I suppose you would say my blind ignorance serves me right. If you have any idea as to how I can reclaim the wreckage of my financial life, please, feel welcome to send me a cosmic sign.

I miss you.

Emma

Agnes brought me up some tea and shortcake biscuits, and from her mouse-like ministrations I sensed she knew something of what was about. She scurried away, and I sat at my desk, staring blankly at the white wall before me.

April 17th

Archibald and I have exchanged notes through Parian and Agnes. We have negotiated a time and a place for the reckoning. At one point throughout the exchanges of the day, Agnes asked if she was to be my second.

"I am not challenging Archibald to a duel, Agnes," I answered, handing her another note. "And if I were to, I certainly wouldn't make you witness the murder."

"Oh, Miss!" And her eyes went wide.

"Never fear, Agnes. Archibald Flat will live to cheat another day."

"I just think it would be much better if, rather than shooting him and being hanged, you poisoned him instead."

"Agnes!"

"I didn't mean— It's only that Parian said—"

"Never you mind what Parian says. Ever! Do you hear me? Now, deliver this note and get back to your work."

I looked as stern as I was able until I could hear her on the lower stairs, and then three days of uncertainty came pouring out of me in a fit of laughter, which continued for a quarter of an hour. Perhaps Agnes's suggestion of poison is what will save Cousin Archibald's life in the end.

The meeting is set for the morning of the 19th, in the unused salon, at ten o'clock.

Time will tell who walks out alive.

April 18th

I just returned from inspecting Lapis Lazuli Minor. Having forced Parian to give up the key, and consequently discovering he had set up a distillery in the small half-patched kitchen, I deem the place mostly livable.

Lapis Lazuli Minor Came To Be Like So: Cousin Archibald attended a lecture years ago where the idea was put forth that the next generation of gentlemen were going to be businessmen. It filled Cousin Archibald with a good deal of verve, and he decided then and there to put into motion a madcap plan. He would divide Lapis Lazuli House and rent the smaller half to a respectable person with deep pockets.

Now, Lapis Lazuli is a good house—it may even be called a fine house—but it was very tall and trim to begin with. There is not much that could be comfortably taken off the waist, so to speak. As I mentioned before, this did not deter Cousin Archibald.

He took a ten-foot slice from the entire north side of Lapis Lazuli House and simply built a wall upwards. Afterward, he had a front door installed where a window used to be. The servant stairs, which took up three of those ten feet, were carpeted, and the very thin rooms were given a few finishing touches. The result being the oddest slice of London to ever be found.

Luckily, there are three fireplaces between the five floors, and a window for each room. This was a fine idea in theory, especially if he were careful to only rent to very thin individuals. But when it was time to build the wall in the garret, a magnanimous spirit overcame Cousin Archibald. He decided to give his future renter an equal half of the garret, which is how the centre window came to be divided right down the middle. Whoever constructed the wall deserves full marks. It was trimmed out nicely. And I can sit in the small window seat and push open my side of the window as the centre bar is now permanently in place. I suppose if someone on the other side opened their window, we could pass notes or biscuits or books back and forth quite companionably. As it stands, Lapis Lazuli Minor—as it was christened by my father, much to my cousin's chagrin—is empty. Archibald's attempts to rent it out over the years have fallen quite flat, no pun on his surname intended. The first renter was a man in a nice suit who insisted he had several sisters to support who would be joining him soon. Cousin Archibald was eager to rent to this man of good repute until a neighbour pointed out, upon the arrival of several made-up and underdressed sisters, that the man was rather of ill repute. There was quite a flutter in St. Crispian's until the misunderstanding was cleared up. Archibald was so embarrassed he would not leave the house for three months.

I was only nine and was not meant to overhear or understand, but as my father was laughing about it for a good half month, the story of Cousin Archibald and his Ladies of the Night just spilled out. My mother blushed. "Declan! Your daughter is listening!"

"And now she'll know better than to be such a fool."

Poor Cousin Archibald.

Since that blessed event, Cousin Archibald has had few renters, none staying long. Needless to say, not many wish to live in ten feet of Lapis Lazuli, no matter how blue the door.

But to find the right tenant?

While the flat is absurdly narrow, certainly a gentleman who keeps the unearthly hours of a sturdy gambling habit should be quite comfortable. I'm not looking for a dissolute tenant. Those tend to prefer the rooms on Traitors Road, by any measure. No, I wish for someone responsible enough to pay rent, but a few unscrupulous habits would suit for keeping him out and about London.

April 19th

Cousin Archibald and I met in the salon. Agnes had cleaned the room, then brought in tea and scones, and as it was raining, Parian saw to the fire. They left us after exchanging a glance hoping for their mutual survival. Once we were alone, I straightened my shoulders and offered my opening parry.

"Cousin Archibald, you have wronged me."

"You scarred my face," he answered, rather primly.

"Oh, for heaven's sake! I threw an empty teapot at you for calling me a beggar who was no better than my bastard Irish father! My father! Who gave you nothing but kindness. You deserved a scar and more, you snivelling rat."

It took me a moment to catch my breath after such a speech. We were both taken aback, but in an odd way it seemed to clear the air. Archibald had the good grace to flush a deep purple and said, "I will write to Matilde and demand your three years' salary. Silver or no silver."

"You most certainly will."

"I will also hand over the household books, as you wish to keep the accounts."

"Please do."

"And here are my last outstanding debts. It cannot be said that Archibald Flat doesn't mostly pay his creditors on time."

I glared as he set the papers down between us.

He was wringing his hands on his lap when he looked me fully in the eyes for the first time since—well, perhaps ever. "You should not say the word bastard, Emma. Your mother would not have approved, and she was a lovely woman. You are not much like her."

I bit back the rueful twist of my lips, certain he was attempting a compliment, however mismanaged. "I was only quoting what you said to make me so angry. My father was very good to you."

"For an Irishman," Archibald answered with a shrug.

"You are ridiculous!"

He tilted and brushed his wispy hair aside so I could see The Scar, a conversation I would not indulge again.

"Let us return to our business. We need to figure a way not only to keep Lapis Lazuli House but also pay Parian and Agnes. Now, I was over at Lapis Lazuli Minor yesterday, and I think we must create a small income by letting it out. Do you know the best way to secure a reliable tenant?"

"As a matter of fact," Archibald sniffed, "the man who owns the gentleman's glove shop down the lane has a friend returning to London who needs a place to stay. He enquired if I would consider offering the accommodations of Lapis Lazuli Minor."

The thought of Archibald having a hand in who would live next door was the dourest option possible. I could picture the poor fool eager to broker a deal with Archibald. He would be a dandy dresser with greasy hair and a wet nose. As sorely tempted as I was to ban the notion altogether, I asked, "Is he a good sort of man?"

"Do you doubt my ability to judge character?"

"Possibly."

"Apparently, the prospective renter has been abroad since he was a very young man," Cousin Archibald said. "I've not ever met him personally of course, but this Chambers fellow says he's a good man, although with some unusual views. But I can't think they would be so radical as to make him unsuitable for our purposes. Even people with *views* have money."

"There is nothing wrong with a *view*, unless it's in support of cannibalism; then we might find ourselves in mortal danger," I replied.

Archibald glared. "Shall I engage him?"

"I suppose," I answered, waving a hand. "Yes, as he is in need. The sooner we have a small rent coming, the better for all of us. We have one stoic year to avoid imminent demise."

"Allow me to arrange everything. He arrives in London next week. I believe we could have him settled immediately upon his arrival."

"What would he be willing to pay?"

Cousin Archibald cleared his throat, then said, "You are not a proper young lady."

"Alas." Then, not knowing the root of his statement, I asked, "Why not?"

"Talking about money as if it is a thing to be spoken of. It's shameful the way you pound on doors and throw around sums. Appalling. I am quite embarrassed for you." When my only response was a pointed silence, he continued, "I was thinking this sum would answer." After scribbling with pencil on a sheet of paper, he slid it across the table to me. I looked at the figure and frowned.

"I have no way of knowing if this is too much or too little."

"It is a fair price."

I sighed. "It is something, but not enough. Can you think of any means to supplement our expenses? Could you sell some of your morning robes?"

Archibald gave an indignant sputter. "Why, I never— Have I asked you to sell your hair? What do you take me for? Some cheap beggar?"

Yes, in truth, I do.

Not desirous for another pugilistic round, I dismissed him. "By all means, rent Lapis Lazuli Minor. Now go. We are through here."

With a nod, Cousin Archibald stood, pocketed two scones, and disappeared.

April 20th

Arabella came for tea. She arrived in a fine carriage and stepped out like she was on a cloud. I waved from my window and pantomimed she join me upstairs. When she ascended all five flights, without so much as a short breath, she reclined gracefully in one of my old chairs.

"I have a surprise for you, Emma," she said. "I've instructed your man to bring it up. You will love me forever."

Agnes brought the tea and was leaving just as Parian's heavy footfalls were heard on the stairs. When he arrived, gasping, he had a small trunk in his arms. But instead of complaining, he smiled dutifully towards Arabella. "Is this where you'd like it, Miss?" he said through the pain of such strenuous work.

"Just so. Thank you, Parian."

Parian set the trunk down and, with a nod towards Arabella and a grunt towards me, left us to ourselves.

"I really have no idea what you've done to the poor man to have him treat you so," she said, taking off her gloves.

"Nor I."

"I blame your lovely Irish father."

Casting my eyes heavenward a moment, I offered Arabella a cup of tea and then asked, "What is in the trunk?"

Now Arabella smiled. "Do you remember those few belongings of your parents we hid at Spencer Court? I've had them brought down without Mama knowing. They're in the trunk."

"You managed it already!"

"I did. You've been without them long enough, and now that you've a permanent home..."

I was on the floor opening the trunk before she could tell me to wait.

There were things I didn't even remember. A shawl of my mother's. A vase. A packet of the letters my parents had exchanged between themselves. My mother's wedding ring. A small mirror. Her Bible. And there in the bottom, wrapped in a blanket, was my father's illustrated Shakespeare. The complete works with each of his illustrations pasted into the binding. I lifted it up and held it to my chest.

"You managed it already," I repeated, softer this time as my heart was beating so hard in my chest I could hardly speak. "Arabella."

"Don't look at them now. I'm here for only an hour before I must report to Mother and my dancing instructor. Go through them when I'm gone and you've some privacy."

Standing, I placed my father's Shakespeare and my mother's Bible on the green bookshelf and went back to sit in the chair near Arabella's, gazing fondly across the room.

"Now I'll never have your attention. You're worse than a girl just out of the schoolroom at her first ball."

I smiled and gave my cousin a cheeky expression. "You only attended your first ball last year."

"Yes, but we can both agree, I hardly have the composure of a girl just out of the schoolroom. I am too sophisticated for that."

Yes, she is.

"Tell me, Emma, what you have been doing with your freedom?"

After speaking of the neighbourhood, I finally declared the truth of my soon-to-be-impoverished state. I tried to deliver the news as a comic tragedy in three acts, but Arabella did not laugh. Her stronger emotions were expertly schooled, but her eyes sparked as I spoke of Archibald's deplorable actions.

"The villain."

"Quite."

"How is it possible he could have done such a thing? Legally, I mean. We both know he's a self-serving creature."

"Father authorized Archibald's use of all accounts, giving him legal access until I reached my majority."

Arabella shook her head with the same disapproval as Mr. Penury. "I loved my uncle, Emma, but his tendency as a dreamer more than once left him a fool."

"Arabella!"

"We both know it's true. However lovely he was."

She was right, in part. Yet I wished to say it wasn't foolishness; it was an ability to live his own life without need for more. He so very often found Archibald nothing more than an absurdity, I suppose he never thought the man would do any real harm.

"What's done is done," I sighed.

"Pity you're too stubborn to accept my promise that my husband and I will take care of you," Arabella answered lightly. "You would have nothing to worry about if you did."

"You don't even have a husband," I countered. "Your mother won't see you engaged before next Season, and by the time you marry, I'll be in the gutter. Pride or no pride, I need to survive now."

"Ask Mother for money."

"She would make me sell the house before giving me a penny."

"True. Will you find a position?" she said, unsuccessfully attempting not to cringe.

"I am considering all possible courses, though I'm not certain any work I could find would help me keep up with expenses, especially as we've two salaries to pay."

"Let Parian go."

I laughed.

As she was leaving, Arabella handed me a small envelope. "Five pounds to see you well fed."

"I won't accept charity," I answered, trying to give it back.

"Says the girl who is having an entirely new wardrobe made on her aunt's account. Keep a few pounds in case of emergency and spend the rest. Oh, Phineas and Oliver Brookstone write hello, and look forward to seeing you once Mother calls you to the front lines."

"Ah, yes. Well, send them my best."

"I will."

I didn't read any of the letters. I'm not ready. But I folded the blanket across my bed, placed the hand mirror and vase on the wash table, and hung the shawl—a soft pink and green—on a hook behind the door. Then I pulled the Bible and Shakespeare from the shelf and opened the first. The Bible had Father's name, Mother's name, then mine, written in her hand. It was worn and small enough to fit inside a reticule. Shakespeare was another matter. It was the complete works, and he by no means was going to be carted around. Opening the front cover, I was greeted with a full illustration featuring many of Shakespeare's characters. There was Henry V inspiring his men on to the Battle of Agincourt. Oberon and Titania. The prince, Benedick, and Claudio. Lear as a beggar on the cliffs. Brutus holding a knife behind his back. Ophelia staring blankly at the sky from her watery grave. Father's deft hand giving them life with a few lines of ink and watercolour, just as his voice had done the same when he read the plays aloud to me. Seeing his work again was such a tremendous shock, I closed the book.

I will relish every page, but I will take time. I will read them through slowly, stretching the delight as far as I can.

Later

Opening it once more just now, it fell open to *The Tempest*, with an illustration of Prospero and Miranda, Ariel whispering in his ear.

This is where I will begin, on an enchanted island free from the worries of this world.

April 22nd

The mice have not been deterred. No matter how I stuff the holes, another appears as if by cursed magic. Agnes suggested I fill a glass bottle with bread crumbs. She said that the mouse would squeeze its way into the bottle and eat and eat and eat. "It will grow too fat to skinny itself back out again, and then you could take the mouse out to the back garden and smash it."

Sounds barbaric, but it may be worth a try.

April 23rd

I received a letter from Evelyn today. I honestly have no idea what to make of it. He has not written since Maxwell's death.

Emma,

You know I've never been one to write letters. I've not the patience to get it all out. You may guess I am not writing only to ascertain if you are well. Clearly, I hope you are. If you weren't, you know you could write to me for assistance. We did not part on the best of terms, but we've been solid friends for a good many years now and the words that passed between us do not alter that.

Emma, I'm writing to tell you that my father is considering exhuming Maxwell's grave that he might bury his remains here at Barrows Edge. I don't know if it will happen—you know how Father is; blusters north one minute, only to bluster south in the next. But I felt you should be prepared, or at very least warned, if the course holds true and he is willing to bring my brother home from that godforsaken place.

I wish he would leave it well enough alone. It's been a miserable three years—Mother on the edge of herself, Father raging or sentimental, worse when he combines the two. But perhaps it would be a blessed relief to see Maxwell come home.

For better or for worse, there is your warning shot across the bow. I'd rather you hear it from me than read about it in the papers. No need to reply unless you have something specific to relay to me. I promise to write when there are any developments which would merit your attention.

Maxwell would want you to know. The two of you were close. I recognise that, despite what I said and what I accused you of.

It was unjust. There. How's that for an apology? I managed to scrape one together at the very end of a letter doing nothing more than raising hopes of another depressing memorial service. I really am a beast.

Regards,
Evelyn

I read the letter three times over, then folded it up, only to tap it against the corner of the desk while I came to terms with everything he said.

Admittedly, the thought of a burial service seems…difficult. But Maxwell would love to be home. Green grass, fields, the slow creek between the trees. And if the hours we spent talking in the church yard are any indication, he will be happy to be laid at rest there. If he bothers to come back to this silly earth and look at it at all.

Three years is a long time. He could have travelled far beyond any of us by now. I once asked him about the afterlife. I said, "Maxwell, what do you think it will be like?"

He answered back, "Well, Lion, I can't rightly say, but I do hope I'll know better what to do with that one than I do with the one I've got at present."

It was not long after he was for the army. And I wish we had known it then, saying goodbye, that he would be killed in the desert of Afghanistan. People say they are glad they never knew their last moment together. Oh, but I wish I'd known it then. It's not on account of my bravery, but rather his. Maxwell would not have been scared. He would have leaned against the stone wall and said, "Well, Lion, I'm off, and it looks like this will be the last I see of this green place."

And I would have felt the collapse of my heart no less keenly than when I did finally hear the news, but he would have been beside me. Those grey eyes looking at me right up until the point when my heart remembered it had to keep me alive for several more years yet. And once I'd recovered—not from the bitter truth, but from thinking it would take me down with him—he would have lifted his chin and given me that sought after mark of his approbation: the single nod, followed by a smile braced with as much determination as he could manage.

While there are many things beyond our control, I've always thought the cruellest is that we mortals are not told when our last glance is just that.

I almost went to sleep without lighting a candle for Father, the letter heavy on my mind. But just before bed I remembered, and am now curled up on the window seat with my burning candle, the window open to the spring night, believing there must be worse sorrows than losing my mother and my father, and the only boy who ever made up a beating part of my heart. Only I can't think of any.

April 24th

After my morning walk, I took Arabella's five-pound note and went down to the Reed and Rite. After purchasing paper, ink, envelopes, a few new nibs, and feeling I could spare a few coins, I went downstairs for coffee and whatever tea cakes they could throw at me. I consumed my edible wares slowly. Sitting in the corner, I had a good view of those inside, as well as those walking out on the street. Mr. Green came in and, upon seeing me in the corner, came over and welcomed me home.

"There have been reports you're back with us. Jolly good that you are! A miracle, that," he said, as if I'd returned from the dead. "When word got round you were in Bournemouth, well, we none of us thought you would make it out alive. Few people do, you know."

"I very nearly didn't," I laughed. "But I'm here now, for keeps."

"Good, good! I'll tell the Missus. She'll visit or send round a few of her jam dodgers."

"I would welcome both."

"But especially the latter, am I right?"

He was.

April 25th

Agnes came rushing into the garret tonight, after I'd already gone to sleep.

"Miss Lion! I was in the garden and there he was! It was only to take some water out to the back garden, I swear it. I didn't mean for it to happen!"

"What are you talking about? Agnes, stop screaming and tell me who was in the garden. Are you well?" I had lit a candle by this point, so I could see the trembling maid holding a hand to her heart, eyes wide as a cartwheel coin.

"I saw him, Miss, clear as day."

"Who?"

"The Roman."

"The Roman!" I grabbed her hand and pulled her into the dark, crowded west garret. We slipped through the furniture and peeked out of the window.

"Where was he? I cannot see anything."

"He was standing right there." And she pointed to the overgrown rose shrub beside the brick patio. "I went out of that door there and started so badly upon seeing him, I spilled half the bucket of water on myself."

"And?" I prodded, gesturing her to continue.

"And he looked right at me, but dinna move." The Scottish accent that her mother had taken such pains to beat out of her was flowering in fine fashion.

"Then?"

"He kept looking at the window next to this, the garret window in the other part of the house."

"Lapis Lazuli Minor?"

"He just stared and stared. And then he said, 'A man of war comes to this house.' And then I squealed, and then he was gone."

"And then?" I added dryly, a poor attempt to counter the chills along the back of my neck.

"And then I came in screaming for you. I'll not sleep a thousand nights now, Miss Lion. Don't make me sleep alone behind the kitchens."

"Nonsense, Agnes. He sounds like a perfectly amiable ghost."

"He was, for all that. He didn't look at me cross-eyed or laugh or anything, but who is the man of war? Why will he come here? Will he burn us all down?"

At this point, any supernatural fear was forced from the room by the comedy of Agnes.

"Really, Agnes. One simply cannot go around thinking an old Roman ghost knows two ends of every stick."

"Wouldn't he know a lot more than us?"

She had a point, but I was not going to indulge any irrational fear at quarter to midnight. "Go to bed, Agnes. There has never been an ill report of The Roman in all of St. Crispian's. We should take it as a comfort he spent some time in our garden."

"But do you think the man Mr. Flat is renting the other part of the house to is the man of war?"

"We do not even know what that means. He could have declared a war on foxes in the countryside, for all we know. I'm not going to follow your silly speculations at this time of night. Now go down to your room. You will be perfectly safe. And when our tenant arrives, he will be perfectly normal."

I sounded more confident than I felt; one of the great secrets to life. Yet, after Agnes went downstairs, I stayed in the west garret, staring into the garden, wondering what The Roman could possibly mean. To my blind relief and utter disappointment, he did not reappear. After an hour, I finally returned here to my room but cannot settle. Sleep is yet a far way off.

April 26th

A few hours ago as I was sitting in my window, having just opened to the first act of *The Tempest*, a hansom cab, followed by a wagon full of trunks and oddly shaped boxes, stopped in front of the house. For a moment there was no action save the two drivers getting down and motioning to the three largest trunks in the back of the wagon. Then the door of the cab opened. A man stepped down. He was tall, broad shouldered, with a rather unkempt beard, and I couldn't help but think of the sailors in *The Tempest* who had crashed upon the shore of a mysterious island. The way the man looked about him, up Whereabouts Lane and down it, he may have been thinking the same. As he walked round the back to the drivers, it was with a pronounced limp.

Cousin Archibald appeared then like Prospero himself, welcoming the stranger to the island of Lapis Lazuli. (I, myself, would give him the role of Caliban.) When Archibald extended his hand, he was given a handshake in return by the stranger. They spoke for a few minutes more—meaning Cousin Archibald prattled away while the man stood patiently, trying to give relief to his injured leg without calling attention to it.

"Let the man alone, Cousin," I whispered to the glass. "Can't you see he's unwell?"

Be it fate or angels or Ariel himself, my plea was heard. Archibald nodded, handed the stranger a key, and waved as he ascended the stairs, closing the door behind him. Even through five floors, I would swear I could hear Archibald whistling with self-satisfaction.

I watched the stranger as he walked up the stairs of Lapis Lazuli Minor, unlocked the door, then gave orders to the drivers. Limp notwithstanding, he helped carry in all the trunks and odd-sized boxes. Finally, he paid the drivers and disappeared inside the door.

Less than a quarter of an hour later I heard someone on the steps and then a crash on the other side of the garret wall. It so startled me I almost dropped Shakespeare on his head. There were footsteps on the stairs again. For the next hour I heard him going up and down, that strange halt of his limp translating into the echoes. I cannot be certain, but it sounds as if he is setting up his personal bedroom on his side of the garret. I moved around quietly, afraid to make noise, not wanting to intrude somehow. Strange as it sounds, the man seems to be owed rest by some intangible law.

I went out for a long walk, first canvassing St. Crispian's then walking Primrose Hill. There were dark clouds gathering in the south, although the sun shone over my piece of London. I thought of Gonzalo in the first pages of *The Tempest*, who answers when he's told to get off the deck and allow the sailors room to do their work in the storm, "Nay, good, be patient."

To which the Boatswain replies, "When the sea is!"

I don't know why the words repeated themselves in my mind. Perhaps that is what I feel about my precarious place in life. Be patient, says every voice of reason. When the sea is! I wish to yell back. Until my world feels solid beneath my feet, my life feels attacked by the rush and tumble of every uncertain wave. And this stranger who has now washed upon our shore makes me feel both melancholy and impatient. I cannot understand why.

Later

The walls between my garret and the stranger's do not hold many secrets. I know he's aware of me now, for when I returned from my walk, I heard him pause at the sound of my door closing; then he cautiously continued to sort whatever he was sorting. After an hour I could hear a washbasin, then more trunks opening. Someone called up the stairs then, coming up to greet our tenant. Perhaps the man who owns the glove shop came to see his friend settled? To my relief, I could hear the rise and fall of intonation but not the actual words. This meant my own privacy was assured. His friend did not stay, and it wasn't long before I heard a sigh and then no sound at all. I think he had fallen asleep.

Come evening, when it was growing dark, the clouds continuing to build and a wind rising, I heard the tenant leave the garret. Curiosity being one of my taskmasters, I stayed where I was in the window seat and looked down into the evening, a streetlamp shining in the fading light. The front door of Lapis Lazuli Minor opened, and the new tenant stepped out onto the stoop.

He was clean shaven and in full evening dress—scarcely looked like the man who had entered hours before. But his limp persisted as he made his way down the stairs and onto the pavement. Then he paused under the lamplight and inexplicably looked directly up at my window. There I was, my temple pressed against the glass, unabashedly watching.

Our eyes met.

He appears to be a younger man, perhaps thirty? His face was shadowed, but seemed sharp, angled, like he has gone rather peckish too many times, but not for food. I can't explain it. Only I felt like the storm building in the night sky was a harbinger of this man standing alone in the street.

Neither of us had the good grace to look away. We simply stared as long as our curiosity demanded. After his prolonged gaze, followed by the slight narrowing of his eyes, he lifted a hand to his hat and tipped it, just as the first drops of rain pelted my window. Then he disappeared down Whereabouts Lane.

April 27th

Cousin Archibald left town this morning. Agnes told me he was going, otherwise I would have missed him entirely. (Missed his leaving that is, not his person.)

"I'm going to see Matilde and settle your salary in person. I intend to stay a few days, perhaps a week," he told me as he was putting on his gloves and arranging his hat. My gallant knight, off to fight the dragon so as to ensure he wouldn't end up on the street. It's inspiring to see how much concern he has for recovering my owed money when he needs it to live on.

"Is Parian going with you?"

"Dear me, no. He's already left to visit his brother."

Agnes and I exchanged a look of joint approval.

"Enjoy your visit, Cousin," I said, smiling. "Lapis Lazuli is in our good hands."

"That brings me little comfort, Cousin," he retorted. "And don't bother our new tenant. He's a busy man and has no need for women flocking about his personal business."

"What a disappointment," I answered. "I was going to henpeck him until he cried."

"Your humour is never appreciated in this house." Those were his final words before he departed. I almost called after him that I understood that fact quite well.

Cousin Archibald took not one carrying case, but two. The second, Agnes told me later, was filled only with silk morning coats.

Agnes celebrated by retiring to the kitchen to bake sweet biscuits. I, freed from my tower with the absence of Cousin Archibald, took Shakespeare to the drawing room and fully reclined on the sofa. It wasn't long before a sweet smell wafted in from the kitchen and Agnes followed with a plate of biscuits and tea.

"Bless you, Agnes. That smells divine."

"I made double, to celebrate."

It was then the idea struck me. "Agnes? Why don't you take some biscuits over to our tenant?"

She paled. "Oh, never, Miss Lion."

"Whyever not?"

"Because The Roman said he was a man of war."

"You don't know exactly what he meant by that."

"Still."

"He limps. Did you see him? Think how uncomfortable it will be for him to go down to the Reed and Rite when he needs something good to eat, limping all the way. We don't even know if he has a cook. Knock on his door, hand him the plate, then return and tell me everything."

"I can't."

"You can. I'll give you all day tomorrow off, if you do."

"You mean it?"

"Certainly. Do whatever you like and sleep in on Sunday."

She weighed this delight against the dread of facing the unknown warmonger of a tenant. "All right then, Miss Lion, I'll take him a plate."

"Wonderful! Pay attention to everything about him. I expect a full report."

I waited inside while she walked from our front door to his. She knocked and we waited. Nary a sound. She knocked again. She knocked a third time. Finally, when I had poked my head out of the door and we'd shared a shrug, the door of Lapis Lazuli Minor swung open.

I heard a voice ask, "Can I help you?" just as Agnes closed her eyes and thrust the plate towards him. "I made extra biscuits and we brought you some because you must be a nice kind of man no matter what The Roman said so I hope you enjoy them and I'll see you again but not tomorrow because I'm going to Piccadilly Circus." Then she finally took a breath.

It was against human capacity not to laugh at such a display. It burst from me and rang off the building against the street. Before I could clap my hand over my mouth, Agnes had shoved the plate into the hands of our tenant and run round to our front door, slamming it behind her as I fell back into the hall, still laughing.

"I—what did I say?" she said.

I shook my head, tears running down my face. "It was a lovely monologue, Agnes, it really was."

"He looked at me like I was daft."

"Never. Did you get a good look at his face?"

Agnes slid down the door and sat on the floor. "I did at that."

"And?"

"He could catch a rabbit, that one."

"What do you mean?"

Agnes looked up. "I mean, back home the hawks would swoop out of the sky and snatch the rabbits. Good to look at but watch your back. Ya ken?" she asked, the banished Scot rising in her relaxed speech.

"I ken, Agnes. Good work. You've earned your day at Piccadilly Circus."

"I have at that, Miss Lion. I don't think my heart will ever slow down."

"You better put your feet up for the rest of the afternoon," I replied, leaving her to recover from her great act of bravery.

April 28th

I visited Mary at her boarding house this evening. She was busy typing notes for the professor in her small, crowded room, but I convinced her to stop long enough to hear of the stranger now living on the other side of my wall.

"And you know nothing else about him?"

"Nothing."

"How mysterious."

I sighed. "Very. And I have discovered the construction of our joint wall to be lacking, as just left of my desk a sliver of his lamplight shines through after I've extinguished mine," I admitted. "What is the best way to seal it off, do you suppose? Perhaps with paint?"

"Can you see his room through it?"

"Oh no. It's far too thin, but it ought to be sealed nevertheless."

I did not admit, nor do I confess here, if I have made the attempt.

"Miss Lamb would never approve," Mary said, grinning.

"Miss Lamb need never know. Speaking of things Miss Lamb need never know, how's Jack?"

Mary's cheeks pinked.

Now, I have known Mary to have been caught climbing through a window, impersonating a duchess, and stealing the headmistress's spectacles, and she's never so much as looked away in shame.

"You haven't fallen in love with him, have you?"

"Certainly not!" Mary said indignantly. And I believed her. She's never been shy about claiming who has caught her fancy. "It's only that I've met a few of his friends, and I must tell you, Miss Lamb would definitely not approve."

"You haven't gone too wild on me, have you, Mary?"

"Nothing very shameful. A party after a successful play is all. And he taught me how to play cards. At his club. I was dressed as a man."

"Mary!" I gaped. "You didn't!"

She grinned, brushing a stray strand of brown hair away from her face. "I won two hands and walked off with twenty pounds."

"You are the rightful hero of all things, Mary," I said. "I am proud to call you my greatest friend. But if you do it again and get caught—"

"Spare your worry, Emma. Miss Lamb very nearly caught me, and I can't afford to lose my room, let alone either of my positions. Jack knows I'm reformed. For now."

"Stay that way," I answered, looking about the room at the stacks of transcribed notes. "How's your professor?"

Mary shrugged. "I've still never met him in person, but he pays mostly on time and always has a furious number of notes for me to type up and put in some kind of order. I've learned more about the East India Company than I ever wanted to."

I sank back into my chair. "Haven't we all?"

April 29th

Hawkes was not at church today. The entire congregation was at a bit of a loss. There was a vicar serving as a replacement who droned for an impressive length of time. St. Crispian's has not been so inflicted for many years. But we banded together and made it through to the end.

"Do you know where Hawkes has got himself off to?" asked Mrs. Simpkins afterward.

"No idea," I replied. "Would any of his Cambridge friends know?"

"Oh, not a single one showed. Did you notice how reverent the back row was? That's because it was empty."

"Perhaps they all went to the seaside," I answered, not able to see Young Hawkes there at all.

"The seaside," she sighed. "Sounds lovely. Could have taken us all." Then she looked over at me and said, "Miss Lion, your eyes are like the seaside. Sea green and lovely as the day. I've never seen them on anyone else, your father excepting. I wonder where he got them."

"A shop in Dublin, most likely."

"Cheeky girl."

"Thank you, Mrs. Simpkins."

April 30th

I woke this morning to the sound of the tenant getting himself ready for the day. It was early, a faint measure of light coming through the window. I wasn't tired, so I dressed and left the house before Agnes had stirred. Being my last day of freedom before turning slave to Aunt Eugenia's social calendar, I wished as much freedom as possible. After sitting at Jacob's Well for half an hour, I began to walk down Whereabouts just as the tenant was letting himself out of his front door. Far enough up the road, he didn't see me, nor could I really see him, only to note that he glanced up towards my window. He seems to walk a great deal, for a man with a limp.

A small package arrived for me. Upon unwrapping the box, I first found a note.

> *Emma,*
>
> *Here are your calling cards. Be ready to use them at my disposal. Come round tomorrow at eleven o'clock to discuss the social obligations I intend to put you under. Be warned.*
>
> *Your Aunt*

With a deep breath, I looked inside. There they were, stacked perfectly, and removing one of the cards revealed a beautiful lion embossed in gold on the back, standing on his back paws with his front paws raised to fight. I love it. My name and address were foiled in gold on the front. Yet the most surprising detail was the painted edge of the cards. It was in a beautiful sea green, to match my eyes. Say what she will about Affection, but Aunt Eugenia did not order such a card without it, whether Arabella arranged the details or no. Either way, I held the card to my chest, closed my eyes, and took a deep breath. Come hell or high water, I am going to keep this house. And no one will take it from me.

Emma M. Lion
Lapis Lazuli House
London

THE PERSONAL LIBRARY *of* EMMA M. LION
As It Currently Stands

The Complete Works of Shakespeare by *William Shakespeare*
Illustrated by Declan Lion

The Holy Bible

Dear Reader,

As appalling as it is to read another's journal, I would like to thank all those who made it possible for you to begin reading mine.

Thank you to the family and friends of Beth Brower. She has them in abundance, and they are always encouraging and believe in her. Which is the nicest of things. She specifically is grateful for the time given by Caitlin, Jenesse, Kimberly, her mother, her father, Rose, and Alena; their contributions are so very appreciated.

Thank you, Angie, who listened to the madcap plan over a cup of cocoa.

No thanks to Rob.

Thank you, Tyson Cantrell, for allowing your lovely design to grace the cover of my journals.

Thank you, Jennifer Lerud. For your brilliant copy editing, your generosity, and your goodness. I sleep better knowing Beth has you on her side.

Thank you, Allysha Unguren, for your talents and wisdom. For sussing things out. And for weighing curious, singular, and peculiar.

Thank you, Ben Unguren, for all the magician's tricks. And for cleaning Beth's typewriter. And for putting purple ink on the spools. You are a rare combination of the analogue and digital in this degenerate age.

Thank you, Kip. For making the good possible. And for being the best. Beth is a fool if she ever takes you for granted.

A note concerning the presumptuous Beth Brower, who thought it a good idea to put my journals into the world. She lives with the aforementioned Kip, her chemist husband, and their cat, Spy Cat Grey.

Beth enjoys citrus scents, books, handwoven rugs, and walking in any weather. She listens to songs on repeat. She feels rather fiercely about the ones she loves and needs windows for light and walls for art.

Beth Brower has written the following books:

The Queen's Gambit
The Ruby Prince
The Wanderer's Mark

The Q

The Beast of Ten

The Unselected Journals of Emma M. Lion

You can find more information on her website and Instagram.

www.bethbrower.com
@bethbrower

You can also subscribe to Beth's newsletter and find short fiction about the characters of St. Crispian's on Substack.

Beth Brower Scribbles Away
bethbrower.substack.com

The Unselected Journals of Emma M. Lion: Vol. 2 is available now.

Sincerely,
Emma

www.ingramcontent.com/pod-product-compliance
Lightning Source LLC
LaVergne TN
LVHW090031160926
848055LV00001B/2